Join Hercules as he embarks upon heroic
journeys battling ancient gods, mythic creatures
and horrific monsters . . .

HERCULES

THE LEGENDARY JOURNEYS™

*All-new, original adventures from
Boulevard Books!*

BE SURE NOT TO MISS BOULEVARD'S ALL-NEW SERIES
STARRING

XENA

WARRIOR PRINCESS™

HERCULES
THE LEGENDARY JOURNEYS™

BY THE SWORD

A novel by Timothy Boggs
based on the Universal television series
created by Christian Williams

BOULEVARD BOOKS, NEW YORK

HERCULES: THE LEGENDARY JOURNEYS: BY THE SWORD

A novel by Timothy Boggs, based on the Universal television series
HERCULES: THE LEGENDARY JOURNEYS,
created by Christian Williams.
HERCULES: THE LEGENDARY JOURNEYS
™ & © 1996 MCA Television Limited.
All rights reserved. Licensed by MCA/Universal Merchandising, Inc.

A Boulevard Book / published by arrangement with
MCA Publishing Rights, a Division of MCA, Inc.

PRINTING HISTORY
Boulevard edition / October 1996

The Putnam Berkley World Wide Web site address is:
http://www.berkley.com/berkley
Make sure to check out PB Plug, the science fiction/fantasy newsletter, at
http://www.pbplug.com

ISBN: 1-57297-198-3

BOULEVARD
Boulevard Books are published by The Berkley Publishing Group,
200 Madison Avenue, New York, New York 10016.
BOULEVARD and its logo are trademarks
belonging to Berkley Publishing Corporation.

PRINTED IN THE UNITED STATES OF AMERICA

10 9 8 7 6 5 4 3 2 1

For Kevin Sorbo,
who has no idea how much fun he lets me
have each week,
but that's all right, because I have it anyway.

And Ginjer Buchanan,
my brother's favorite editor,
who made the phone call that allowed me to
take that fun
and have it every day by writing this book.

*Life is like a bowl of granola and acorns: it
may be good for you, but the nuts are more fun.*

—LIONEL FENN
(my brother, who says things like that all the time,
which is why we don't let him out very often)

BY THE SWORD

1

The sky was filled with stars and sound. A great wind raced out of the mountains to the north, bending tree-tops and snapping twigs, scattering dead leaves and the remnants of the harvest, chasing summer before it to the edge of the sea.

In the vast forest beyond the village of Markan, there was no light at all save for the sputtering glow of a campfire at the back of a small clearing. Two men huddled over the stone-ringed flames, studiously ignoring the crawling shadows the fire cast on the lower branches. Their clothes were ragged and ill-fitting, singed in a few places that had nothing to do with the fire at hand, and their threadbare hooded cloaks were gathered around them like blankets.

They could hear the wind, and were grateful they couldn't yet feel it; they couldn't see the stars.

"I tell you, I have a bad feeling about this, Trax," the first man said. He was burly and tall, his face and hands scarred by knife and sword. In his left hand he held the slightly overcooked haunch of a scrawny rabbit. The rest of the animal was still on the spit over the flames.

Trax, who was smaller but no less strong, sighed with exaggerated patience. "So? You always have bad feelings, Castus."

"It's my nature."

"And you're usually wrong."

Castus chewed thoughtfully, staring at the flames. "*Usually* doesn't mean all the time."

Trax didn't bother to argue. His friend got that way sometimes, all introspective and contemplative, thinking about things a mere mortal shouldn't concern himself with, especially in a strange place in the middle of a night that shouldn't have been so cold. In Trax's view, living was what counted. As long as you could. Stealing, too, of course, but that was part of living. His living, anyway. And if the gods wouldn't mind a touch of hubris here, he was pretty good at it, too.

The problem was, being a thief, even one with the skills and panache he had, hadn't gotten him very rich. In fact, he thought glumly, rich didn't even enter into it. Bloody poor was more like it.

Until now.

A hand reached out to be sure the bundle that lay

between them was still there. It was long, swathed in thick black leather that shone in the firelight, and securely tied with heavy cord. It had taken them over a week to get it. It had cost them the lives of four of their band.

Of which, unpleasant truth be known, only he and Castus remained.

Castus gnawed the bone to get at the marrow. "You think he'll come?"

"He'll come."

The clearing lay fifteen paces from the woodland trail; they sat at the clearing's back so they could see, or hear, anyone approach.

"You think he'll bring the money?"

"He will."

"A hundred dinars, Trax."

"Gold," the thief corrected with a dreamy smile. "A hundred dinars in pure gold, my friend. And we'll get twice, three times that much from the changers in Sparta if we're lucky. Midas should be so rich."

"You think—"

Trax thumped him impatiently on the top of his head with a loose fist. "Stop it! You think too much. It'll make your head hurt."

"It hurts now."

Trax thumped him again, just for the hell of it. Castus was a lifelong friend; they had been through a lot of adventures together, shared cells and women and

3

too many close calls to count, but there were times—like tonight—when he wanted to thump the man into the ground, just to shut him up. Castus worried at his worries as if they were that stupid rabbit's bone.

Sparks flared from the pit.

The wind soughed.

"I'm going to buy a chariot," Castus announced, and yanked another haunch off the rabbit on the spit.

Trax stared at him in disbelief. "You're what?"

"I'm tired of walking all the time. My feet hurt. When my feet hurt, I can't think straight."

Trax was about to thump him again, but reconsidered when he realized that the man actually had a decent idea for a change. Why sneak into a village, rob the inn or whatever, and have to *run* away? Lately it seemed as if there were at least a dozen men who could run faster than they did, which often led to him getting a thumping of his own, not to mention the kicking and gouging and slapping around.

Half the time, now that he thought about it, he and his cohorts never even made it out of the village.

But a chariot . . . !

"You're a genius," he whispered in reluctant admiration.

"My head hurts."

A chariot would give them an advantage no other thieves in the kingdom had—at least four more feet.

Of course, on the downside, there was the expense.

You had to buy a horse, or the chariot wouldn't work. Then you had to feed the horse, grease the wheels so they wouldn't squeak at night, keep the reins in good repair, cushions in the back in case one of them got lucky. . . . He frowned, then shrugged. No matter. It was better than getting pounded by a dozen angry villagers. That tended to take the spark out of thieving, no question about it.

On the other hand, if the village had a good chariot of its own . . .

"I hear something."

Trax looked up, automatically adjusting his hood to keep his face in shadow.

Someone had left the trail, and was making no effort to conceal his approach.

"You think it's him?" Castus whispered, nervously nibbling on the haunch.

Trax lay a protective hand on the bundle. "If it's not, you'll have to . . . you know."

He shouldn't have worried; his friend already had his dagger in hand, hidden now by the folds of his cloak. Castus thinking was a danger only to himself; Castus fighting with his trusty spiral dagger was a danger to everyone else.

Seconds later a figure broke through the underbrush and entered the clearing. He was tall, wearing thick black leather armor studded with medallions of burnished silver and polished bone. His heavy boots laced up to thighs thick as trunks. His gleaming black cloak rippled. The hilt of his sword caught the fire-light.

He wore no helmet, made no attempt to hide his face.

"Do you have it?" was all he said.

Castus lumbered to his feet, still holding dagger and haunch. "You have to give the password."

The man scoffed. "You can see it's me, you fool."

"The gods have been known to assume human forms."

Trax held the bundle protectively to his chest and rose cautiously, suddenly wishing he were as tall as his friend. He sincerely hoped Castus remembered the password, because he sure didn't.

"The password," Castus repeated, his voice deep, exposing the dagger's blade.

The man lowered his head and shook it slowly. "My feet hurt."

Castus bobbed his head and grinned. "So do mine. I'm going to buy a chariot, you know. If the horse's feet hurt, I won't care."

The man glared. "That's the password, you idiot!"

"Oh." Castus laughed. "Right. I forgot."

I will disappear now, Trax decided; I will find a rabbit hole and I will jump into it and disappear.

"The prize?" the man demanded.

Trax stepped around the fire pit and said boldly, "The reward?"

They stared at each other for several long seconds before the man plucked a small sack from his belt and tossed it to Castus, who caught it against his chest. Trax hesitated, then handed the bundle over, retreating quickly as soon as the man had it.

The man began to unwrap it. "I have to be sure."

"Of course," Trax agreed readily. "You wouldn't want to be cheated."

The man glanced at him. "I am never cheated."

"Of course not. And we wouldn't think of it, would we, Castus?"

"Trax?"

The rope slithered to the ground.

Trax licked his lips impatiently. He wanted to be gone. He wanted to be in Sparta, convert the gold, and be gone. Preferably somewhere a hundred leagues across the sea.

"Trax?"

"What?"

Castus held out his hand. "It's empty."

The leather wrapping dropped to the ground.

"What's empty?"

"The sack. There's no gold, Trax. He didn't give us our gold."

Suddenly the fire pit dimmed as the clearing filled with a brilliant red light.

Oh boy, Trax thought.

Just before he screamed.

2

Markan was a village of fair size and reasonable prosperity. Its businesses were located on three sides of a cobblestone square, while the open, southern side allowed a sweeping view of rich grassland, distant forest, and the towering, now snowcapped mountains beyond, perpetually swathed by pale mist. In the center of the square was an ancient well around which had been set hard-carved, slightly curved stone benches for the comfort of local and traveler alike.

The homes of the village's inhabitants were set primarily behind the square, reached by narrow streets and alleys most felt perfectly safe in walking alone, even at the darkest hour of the stormiest night. There was no fortress wall here; even the farmers and herders in the valley had little fear of raiders and thieves. It wasn't that such bloodthirsty men didn't exist; it was simply that the vigilance of the king's patrols didn't permit them to exist for very long.

Most Markans agreed in public and private that King Arclin was, except for the occasional tax and tithe, a pretty fair man for a king. Like his father before him, he never executed anyone who didn't deserve it, and, like his father, he knew how to throw one hell of a party when the harvest was in.

On this particularly warm afternoon the square was busy and pleasantly noisy. Brightly clothed women gathered at the well for water and gossip, strapping young men gathered at the well for water and the women, some shopped, some haggled, some laughed, and a demented flock of wild-throated children pursued imagined monsters and evil warriors in and out of the area in a manner just shy of chaos.

Comfortably nestled at the north side was the Bull and Bullock Inn. Outside, beneath an overhanging roof of well-kept thatch, the owner had placed a quintet of small tables for use during pleasant weather, or when the air inside grew too stifling. Within were twice that number carefully placed across the constantly swept floor; plus lanterns on the roof posts to keep the large room bright, a long table that served as a bar for those who didn't want to sit at the tables, decorations on the walls, and a barmaid whose beauty had been measured against the best the kingdom had to offer, and not found wanting.

Nikos Veleralus was content.

Business was good, especially now that Markan had taken long strides in establishing itself as a regular stopping place for travelers going south to escape the harsh winter. Nikos had six fair rooms upstairs and a four-stall stable behind the main building, and they were always filled. His barrels of wine and ale were regularly tapped. And his food, while perhaps not the same elegant cuisine as might be served to a king, sufficed to keep a good man's belly filled without complaint. Even now, during that part of the afternoon when the inn was usually empty, a man sat at one of the tables, enjoying the daily special.

Life, in other words, was pretty much perfect.

Except, Nikos noted sourly, for the urchin racing through the doorway.

Nikos couldn't stand urchins. They were short, they were unbearably noisy, their clothes were disgustingly filthy, and they had the tactless habit of pointing out at the tops of their shrill voices that his nose was too big for the rest of his face. Much too big.

This particular one, who couldn't have been more than eight or nine, fell heavily against the bar, gulping for air. "Nose," he gasped breathlessly, his grimy face puffed with exertion. "Nose."

Nikos glared. "What?" he said flatly. Although he wasn't more than average in height and looks, and noteworthy for nothing other than his nose, he had an

11

experienced bartender's grasp of moderately sincere expressions, ranging from sympathy for a man's troubles with his wife or cattle to if-you-cause-any-more-trouble-I'll-belt-you-senseless-with-my-club.

For the urchin he used the tolerant mode, but only because one couldn't belt a child with the club.

"Bones."

Nikos rolled his eyes. "Sorry, lad, but I gave them to the dogs last night. You have to be quicker than that."

The boy shook his head as he tried to catch his breath again, and Nikos shuddered when something fell out and crawled erratically across the floor. "Bones," the boy repeated. His large eyes blinked wildly, his grimy hands fluttered dangerously over the just-cleaned bar. "Bones."

Experience finally suggested that something was wrong. Urchins generally didn't hang around the Bull and Bullock gasping "Bones" every day. "Nose," maybe, and once in a while "Beak," but never "Bones."

He dipped a small cup into a bucket of water, walked around the bar, and sat as he handed the drink to the child. Gingerly. "What bones?" he asked.

The boy drank gratefully, wiped his mouth with his sleeve, and said, "In the forest."

The innkeeper put a thoughtful finger to his chin. "Bones in the forest, eh?"

"Yes."

"Animal bones were they?"

The boy's eyes widened further, and he shook his head vigorously. Luckily, nothing else fell out.

"Oh no. People bones."

Nikos' eyes narrowed in suspicion. "People bones? Are you sure, boy?"

"Oh, yes." The boy gestured feebly toward the door and took a deep breath. "We were playing Hercules, you see, and I was a cyclops and Dorry was Hercules and he chased me into this clearing and I almost got away except he jumped on me, which he wasn't supposed to do because I wasn't supposed to get dirty today, but Dorry didn't know that, so he jumped on me and we fell down and we landed . . . we landed on—"

The boy hiccuped as soon as he ran out of air.

Nikos, who was still lost somewhere back in the just-getting-to-the-clearing part, waited patiently. Smiling as only adults can do when they haven't the faintest idea what a child was talking about but didn't want to admit it.

Then he saw the unmistakable glint of a tear in the corner of the boy's eye.

More accurately, he saw the pale track the tear made through the grime on the boy's face.

"All right, lad, all right," he said gently, putting a hand on the boy's shoulder before he realized what

13

he was doing. "You take it easy, take your time, tell me when you're ready."

"But I already told you!" the boy wailed in exasperation. "We was in the clearing, Dorry jumped on me, we fell on some bones, they were people bones, Dorry got scared and ran home, and so did I."

Nikos blinked in astonishment, squinted, and looked closer, prepared to be appalled.

He was.

"Bestor, is that you?"

The boy, who, as it turns out, was Nikos' son, nodded, and hiccuped, and another tear track began to work its way toward his chin.

"By the gods, boy, you're filthy!"

"We was playing."

"You look like an urchin!"

Bestor lowered his head contritely. "Sorry, Father."

An urgent shout outside distracted Nikos for a moment, just long enough for his son to throw his arms around his waist, bury his face in his chest, and begin to sob. The innkeeper patted the boy's back awkwardly, torn between the realization that his very own son had turned into an urchin when he wasn't looking, and the news that human bones had been discovered in the forest.

He sighed loudly. Life had been a lot simpler when the boy's mother was alive.

Bestor lifted his face. "Father, what shall I do?"

"Take a bath."

The boy gasped in horror.

Nikos scowled, not at the boy's reaction but upon hearing another shout, this one rather frantic, and coming from the square. "Wait here," he ordered as he rose.

"But, Father, the bones!"

Nikos didn't respond. He strode angrily to the doorway, determined to find out who was disturbing his peaceful afternoon. Probably more urchins. The selfsame urchins who had seduced his only son into forgetting his manners, his lessons, his station in life.

He stepped outside just as a woman screamed.

He put a hand to his chest and muttered, "Oh my."

It wasn't urchins.

It was the Corsco brothers.

For well over a year, the two Corsco brothers had, for some unknown reason, made it their profession to terrorize the village whenever they needed a few dinars, some free food, or some illicit recreation. Homes had been damaged, bones and skulls broken, purses snatched, and women defiled. While the Markan men certainly weren't cowards, neither were they, singly or in groups, capable of taking on ill-tempered men whose arms and legs were broad as boulders, and

15

whose strength was such that tables had been split in half with a single one of their blows.

"Oh my," Nikos said again.

The brothers had cornered two women by the well, and the square, in a disturbing fit of self-preservation, had emptied without a fight. Every few seconds a foolhardy man would race in, wave his arms threateningly, and race out again.

The brothers only laughed as they pushed the women back and forth between them.

Then Nikos growled.

The women were Lydia Cember and her younger sister, Dutricia.

"Father," Bestor exclaimed from the doorway, "look, it's Lydia!"

Nikos nodded grimly. Both he and the boy were in love with Lydia, and she, it appeared, with them. It had been his plan, in fact, to propose a union before the season was over, and he had no doubt she would accept.

"Nikos!"

She had seen him, started to run toward him, and was grabbed from behind by Francus Corsco, who immediately began a disgusting, and loud nuzzling of her neck.

Enraged beyond reason, Nikos whirled, raced inside, reached over the bar, and grabbed the hefty club he used to keep the peace on nights when his customers threatened to become rowdy. He had never actually had to use the thing, just display it, but this was an emergency. He smacked it against his palm and, once outside again, saw that Sinius Corsco had lifted Dutricia onto the well's lip, held her by one arm, and laughingly threatened to shove her over the side. Lydia was on a bench, Francus snorting and pawing hungrily at her skirts.

Nikos howled and charged.

Francus looked up, grinned, and stood.

Nikos swung the club.

Sinius shoved Dutricia into the well, still holding her by her wrist and laughing.

Francus caught the club on its downward swing, wrenched it easily from Nikos' grip, and said with a mirthless laugh, "Die, toad."

Bestor shrieked.

Lydia shrieked.

Dutricia shrieked, her voice echoing a little from within the well.

Nikos wanted desperately to shriek, too, but Francus had one hand around his throat, squeezing mercilessly, while the other rose and fell as it measured the distance between the club and his skull.

"Toad," Corsco whispered.

Nikos could barely see. Most of his air was gone, the bright sun had begun to dim alarmingly, and all he could hear was the blood bellowing in his skull,

Lydia bellowing on the bench, and, oddly, a man's amazingly calm voice say, "I'm trying to eat, do you mind?"

Suddenly the innkeeper was free. His knees buckled instantly and he sprawled on the ground, shading his eyes just in time to see the man from the inn snatch the club out of Francus' hand and toss it away, take Francus by the tunic and toss him away, step over the bench, grab Sinius by the scruff and toss him away while, at the same time, grabbing Dutricia's arm and hauling her safely out of the well.

It takes longer than that for a bird to blink.

The square was silent.

Finally Nikos pushed himself groaning to his hands and knees, glanced around fearfully, and gaped when he saw Francus lying motionless atop the wreckage of one of the inn's outside tables, Sinius lying motionless atop him. A faint cloud of dust drifted over their backs and heads.

He looked at the stranger.

The stranger smiled as he assisted the two shaken women to a bench, sat them down, whispered something, and turned. "Are you all right, innkeeper?"

Nikos nodded mutely.

One by one the villagers returned, whispering among themselves, trying and failing not to stare at the stranger who had saved their women.

The man extended a hand and hauled Nikos effortlessly to his feet. Nikos nodded his thanks and dropped onto the bench beside Lydia, who immediately threw her arms around his neck and began to sob in relief. A moment later Bestor was on his other side, a trembling hand on his father's leg while he stared up at the man.

"Wow," the boy said.

"Thanks," the man answered.

He was fairly handsome in a smoothly rugged sort of way, if, Nikos thought, you liked that sort of thing, which women tended to these days. Long light brown hair parted in the center and neatly brushed to the shoulders, nice eyes, a friendly smile, arms that bulged but didn't brag, a yellowish shirt open to expose a chest that bespoke strength but, like the arms, was too modest to brag. He even had a nose that fit the rest of his face.

"I—" Nikos coughed and massaged his injured throat. "We owe you our lives, sir."

"You were doing just fine. I just kind of butted in, that's all."

Nikos blushed at the polite lie even as Lydia stirred against him.

"Mister?" Bestor tugged at the man's vest. "Can you show me how to do that?"

The man's smile broadened. "I don't think so, son."

"Your name," Nikos said hoarsely, abruptly remembering his manners. "To thank you properly, we really should know your name."

This time it was the man's turn to appear uncomfortable. He shrugged one shoulder, scratched his neck, sighed.

"Hercules," he said at last.

Bestor gasped.

Lydia and Dutricia gasped.

Nikos gasped, but that was because his throat still hurt and Lydia's arms had tightened convulsively around his neck.

Before he had a chance to say anything, however, Hercules turned to the boy and said, "So what's all this about bones in the forest?"

3

Hercules stood at the edge of the forest and wondered just what he thought he was doing. Finding bones in places like this wasn't unusual. People died, animals died, and the natural process produced the obvious. It wasn't as if these people had never seen bones before.

Yet the boy had been so upset, and the father so grateful for the assistance, that before he could stop himself he had promised he would take a look. After all, what harm could it do? Go in, find the bones, see the bones, return to the village, and tell them there was nothing strange going on.

He glanced at the sky then, and sighed heavily, because "nothing strange going on" was not, by any stretch of the imagination, the way to describe what usually happened when he was around.

"What's the matter?"

Nikos stood beside him, his club in one hand.

"Just thinking."

The innkeeper, who had volunteered to accompany him, shifted nervously, and Hercules smiled to himself. Nikos was evidently a good father, and clearly a respected man of the village, who absolutely did not want to be here. The club twitched like a cat's tail, his gaze was unsteady, and a single "Boo!" would probably send him on a record-breaking footrace for home. On the other hand, after he'd been bested by those men, he had to prove to his son and the slender, fair-haired woman named Lydia that he was no coward.

Hercules suspected they knew that already, from the way Nikos had dared take on the Corsco brothers on his own.

It was the father who needed the convincing.

Hercules knew that all too well.

"Where is this clearing?"

They had followed the main road that led out of Markan from the square, left it at an intersection, and continued across the grass toward the woods. Nikos pointed to a faint trail that wound around some high shrubs and saplings and then into the trees. "In there somewhere. He said it's a little off the main path, marked by a big tree split in half by lightning." He squinted at the sun. "Are you sure we have to do this? He won't know if we don't do it."

"No, but we will," Hercules told him gently, and Nikos sighed at the truth of it.

Fifteen minutes later they reached the woodland's main path, but despite the sparse underbrush, finding the tree and the clearing took them another hour.

The only way they knew the clearing was the right one was the fact that they could see the bones.

"Oh . . . my," Nikos said, the club swinging at his side, his weight shifting from one foot to the other.

Hercules slowly walked the perimeter of the clearing, Nikos close behind, skittish and looking everywhere but at the skeletal remains. The foliage overhead kept the area in shifting shade, and the air was cool and smelled faintly of smoke.

"At night," Hercules said, "you can probably see the village lights from the path."

Nikos nodded; it was a fair assumption.

Hercules pointed at the shallow fire pit, and the spit still straddling it. "Either they didn't want to be seen, or they didn't want to come into the village."

"Bandits."

"Maybe. Let's take a closer look."

He returned to the spot where they had entered the clearing. Not five feet away was the first skeleton. Or what was left of it. It was sprawled on its back—a dusty skull with jaw agape, a shattered rib cage with one arm attached, and the pelvic bone, only the left leg remaining, and that only to the knee. By the way it was twisted, this must have been the pile the kids had fallen on.

"Well," said Nikos carefully, "by the looks of them, gnawed and such, they've been here for quite a while. Probably a couple or so months." He scanned the clearing again, partially closing one eye in concentration. "Funny, though, that they haven't been found before this." He gestured vaguely toward the path behind the trail. "We're not exactly that far off the beaten track here."

Hercules hunkered down with a short stick in his hand. He poked at the skeleton, disturbing the femur, frowning when the bone nearly vanished into dust; he poked at the ground around it, shifting blades of grass and dead leaves. Finally he said, "Look."

"Bones," Nikos confirmed without moving.

Hercules glanced up at him. "Closer, Nikos, closer."

Reluctantly the innkeeper knelt beside him, not sure what he was supposed to see and his expression telling Hercules that whatever it was, he didn't want to see it anyway. Then his eyes widened a little.

"They look burned."

Hercules nodded, and pointed with the stick. "I don't know how long ago this happened; maybe you're right about the months, but . . ." He frowned, and rubbed a finger across his temple. "You can still see some ashes caught in the grass." Puzzled, he crossed to the second skeleton, this one larger and even less complete. A dagger lay a handsbreadth away. "The same here." He touched a rib with his boot, and it, too, crumbled to dust.

Nikos licked his lips nervously. "Maybe their clothes caught from the fire there." He frowned. "They couldn't put it out and . . ." He shuddered.

Hercules shook his head. "No, I don't think so. If you look closely, you can see the grass is burned only around the bones. If the fire had caught them, they would have rolled around, or run, and we'd see the results. No, Nikos, these men died where they stood. And this was no campfire that did it. This was something much worse."

"But what?"

Hercules had no answer.

He did, though, have a suspicion.

"The way I see it," Nikos said eagerly as they broke from the forest and headed back to the village, "we have two choices here. The first is, whoever they were, they really pissed off the gods and they were zapped. The gods do that sometimes. Miss one lousy rite, use the wrong wine, and they fry you where you stand." An apprehensive glance at the setting sun. "Not that I'm actually complaining, of course. I wouldn't think of it. The gods are the gods after all."

"Nikos . . ."

"Or they were struck by lightning, a freak occurrence, but not unheard of. Storms like that come through here quite often, as a matter of fact."

"Nikos . . ."

"Or there's sorcery involved. You never know where you stand with a sorcerer, you know. I've heard they can have really nasty tempers. He could have hit them with some kind of fireball spell."

"Nikos, look—"

"Or they could have belonged to some very odd religious sect. I've heard about them, too. Maybe they were involved in a ritual that went wrong. Or—"

Hercules grabbed his arm, barely able to contain a grin. "Nikos, I thought there were only two choices."

The innkeeper shrugged helplessly.

"It's okay," Hercules assured him with a light slap to his shoulder. "I've come up with a few theories of my own, and none of them makes very much sense either."

Ahead they could see a line of people waiting anxiously at the square's open edge. Hercules noted for the first time the broken-down carts and small wagons drawn to either side of the opening, as if ready to be pulled together for some kind of protection.

"Hercules?"

"Yes?"

Nikos scratched at his chin, his neck, pushed a hand back through his hair. "I know you're an important man, and I know you have important things to do, but—"

"Nikos, I don't know what I can do about this. All we know is that two people have died."

"Very mysteriously."

Hercules agreed. "But that's all we know. And it doesn't seem to affect your village. There doesn't seem to be any danger."

"A mystery of life, then?"

"Could be."

Nikos looked at him carefully. "Do you believe it?"

Hercules didn't know if he would have lied or not. As it was, his answer was forestalled by a delighted shout as Bestor sprinted up the road toward them. Nikos waved, his chest a little larger, his stride a little longer, and before long they were surrounded by villagers who were clamoring with questions that had no real answers. This, however, did not really bother them. If fact, the mystery of the bones was soon enough replaced by an instant decision to declare a holiday that night in honor of their famous guest.

Hercules could hardly refuse without seeming ungrateful.

Not, he thought later, that he had any real place to go.

Lying on a raised pallet in a tiny room above the inn, hands folded beneath his head, he listened to the

27

preparations below in the square. On a low table beside the pallet a wick burned softly in its shimmering bed of oil. In the thatched roof outside the room's only window, birds were settling down for their evening's rest.

Yet, despite the noise, it was a peaceful time, a time when, on more than one occasion now, he tended to dwell too much on the past.

On the pain that never quite eased.

Without question, his life was a good one. He traveled throughout the many kingdoms, doing his best to help those who needed help, whether it was a simple matter of gaining respite from bullies like the Corsco brothers, or the more complex task of gaining freedom from tyrants.

Or, sometimes, freedom from the capricious tyranny of the gods.

One in particular.

He had good friends, exciting times, and seldom wanted for anything. On those rare occasions when he was in need, it wasn't long before the need was satisfied.

Any man would be more than grateful for a destiny such as his.

The problem was . . . the *curse* was how this destiny had come to be his.

The first strains of sprightly music rose into the night, accompanied by a hint of girlish laughter.

His eyes closed, just for a second, but in that too brief moment he saw the distant face of Deianeira, his wife, and those of his children, Klonus, Aeson, and Ilea.

Lost to him forever.

When the moment was over, they were gone. Again.

And he, as always, as cursed as always, was still alive.

He sat up quickly, scowling as he swung his legs over the pallet's side, angry at the brief sting of self-pity that tormented him at such times. He knew full well that he could not change the past. The present was good, and there was always the future.

Still, in his solitude, there was the pain.

There was always the pain.

A timid knock on the door caused him to raise his head.

"Come in, I won't bite."

It was Lydia's sister, Dutricia, with a small tray in her hand. On it was a plate of steaming meat, some bread, and a goblet. "Nikos thought you might like something," she said shyly. She was a lovely woman, with long black hair and large black eyes. Her dress was simple, hemmed and stitched in bright colors, and around her shoulders she wore an emerald shawl.

He smiled. "I thought there was a feast."

She set the tray on the table. "From the looks of

it, I think you'll be too busy. A lot of people will want to hear stories of the great Hercules. You'll probably not have a chance to grab more than a bite or two the whole evening. By the time it's over, you'll be starving.''

He laughed as he agreed.

''Besides,'' she added, ''I wanted the chance to thank you in person for what you did for me out there.''

''They weren't so tough,'' he said modestly. ''Nikos could have—''

''No.'' She reached down to touch his arm. ''You're very kind, Hercules, but you know that's not true.''

He realized then that her shawl had somehow slipped from her shoulders. He also realized that her shoulders were bare. It didn't take more than a moment to note that bare shoulders tended to indicate a neckline that . . . he wasn't sure of the proper word, but *plunged* seemed to fit fairly well in this case.

He looked into her eyes, and the eyes that looked back were not only grateful, they were dangerous.

''Uh . . .'' He snatched the bread from the tray, thanked her with a look, and took as large a bite as he could without choking himself.

She sat beside him, a finger tracing the bulge of his biceps to the top of his thick leather arm guard. ''I made it myself, you know.''

30

He blinked. "The bread?"

"The dress."

"Lovely." He took another bite. "You're very good."

"Oh yes." Her left eyebrow arched. "So I'm told."

The finger reached the back of his hand, her nail lightly scratching the depressions between each knuckle. One by one.

The music grew a little louder.

Hercules took another bite of bread.

Dutricia leaned closer.

Plunged, he decided, was wrong; and *plummet* was barely adequate.

"You know," she whispered, "sometimes—"

The music stopped in midnote.

And Bestor charged into the room, hiccuped, gasped "Raiders!"—and ran out again.

4

Hercules leaped from the pallet, stopped at the door when Dutricia yelped, and turned just in time to see her slip to the floor. He ran back, helped her up, apologized, and ran out again, following the boy down the dark stairs to the inn below.

The room was empty.

He hurried outside and stopped again.

The square was lighted by a score of torches lashed to high poles. Long tables had been placed around the perimeter and were already laden with food and drink. But the party was over before it had begun.

Nikos, club in one hand, stood on the lip of the well, shouting instructions to at least two dozen lightly armed men. The carts and wagons had already been drawn across the gap. A handful of women were filling buckets with water in anticipation of fire, and

Lydia was well into the task of rounding up loose children and herding them into the streets toward home. The urchins, this time, didn't mind obeying.

Hercules trotted over to the well and tapped Nikos on the leg.

"Raiders?"

"We're doomed!" a man cried from the shadows.

Nikos directed six archers to the roofs on either side of the gap closed by the carts. "Zorin, I'm afraid," he said gravely.

"Zorin?"

Nikos stared. "What, you've never heard of him?"

Hercules shook his head.

For several months, the innkeeper explained quickly, a band of raiders—nay, a veritable army of raiders—led by a mysterious man named Zorin had been roaming the kingdom and its neighbors despite King Arclin's best efforts to stop them. Stories of death and destruction, stolen livestock and kidnapped women, were staples around hearth and bar. And fairly effective for keeping problem kids in line. Although Markan had thus far been spared Zorin's wrath, most people believed it wouldn't be long before they too were hit.

"Doomed!" the shadow man cried.

"Looks like tonight's the night," Nikos concluded ruefully. He pointed over the carts. "They were spotted on the road." He rubbed his hands together. "But we're ready for them."

Hercules looked at the streets that led off the square. "Nikos, I don't want to disappoint you, you've obviously worked hard, but what's to stop them from coming in from the other sides?"

Nikos seemed shocked. "You're kidding."

"No."

"They'd really do something like that?"

"Yes."

Nikos pursed his lips. "Pride," he answered after a moment's careful consideration. "The stories say they're so bold, they never come through the back door. Why should they when they never lose?"

Hercules studied the other routes again, not caring for the prickling at the back of his neck. "What if the stories are wrong?"

"Doomed, doomed, doomed!" cried the shadow man.

Nikos nodded. "That about covers it."

At which point one of the archers waved and yelled, "They're coming!"—and the square fell instantly silent, save for the hissing of the torches, and the whispered "Doom" of the shadow man.

If the stories were true, however, Hercules suspected that all this preparation would be for naught. The villagers might gain temporary advantage, but temporary, in cases like this, usually ended in disaster.

He thought quickly for a moment, then hurried over to the barrier and stared out into the night.

He could see them, marching boldly down the center of the road.

As far as he could tell, there were only nine or ten of them, perhaps a dozen, marching two abreast. They were heavily armed and heavily armored, at least three of them with feathered lances. Torchlight flared off silver studs on helmets and tunics, and the sound of their boots on the hard ground was like the steady beat of a war drum. Each carried a shield wrapped in hide, which, he knew, was designed to hold, not ruin, whatever arrows came their way.

There were more.

He knew it.

Out there beyond the reach of the light was the rest of the band, however big that might be. These men would be used to test the initial defenses, confident that their losses would be minimal. From the way the villager defenders fidgeted, from the way he saw one archer up on the right struggle to nock an arrow, he reckoned Markan didn't have a prayer, no matter what god or goddess happened to be listening.

Still, he couldn't help wondering . . . always the front way? Always the frontal assault?

This was more than arrogance born of skill and success.

This was . . . he frowned . . . downright spooky.

The raiders halted not ten feet from the cart-and-wagon wall, and a clean-shaven man with a horned helmet took a step forward, his unsheathed sword hanging loosely at his side. He lowered his shield and tapped the sword against it.

"You in there," he called sternly. "You don't have to die, you know."

Nikos had moved to the center of the makeshift wall, where two wagons had been backed against each other. He stood at the narrow gap between the wagons' rear wheels. "Then go away."

The bearded raider laughed. "Not likely, my friend. We've come a long way. We want, uh, food, drink, women . . . and, oh yes, all your money. We get that, and we promise not to harm you."

"And the village?" Nikos asked, sweeping a hand behind him.

"Oh." The raider shrugged. "Well, we'll burn that down, of course."

The Markans growled.

The raiders laughed.

Hercules vaulted smoothly into the wagon before him, put his hands on his hips, and said calmly, "No one gets hurt, nothing gets burned."

The leader gaped, looked at his men, looked back, and grinned. "And who says so?"

"I do."

"And who are you?"

"A friend," Hercules answered before Nikos could.

Again the raider grinned. "Well, listen . . . *friend* . . . why don't you go back where you came from and let me and the guy with the big nose do all the talking. My boys are getting restless."

The boys growled.

Nikos growled, albeit not as effectively as the boys, and swung his club.

Hercules only smiled a little regretfully. "Just leave, all right? I promise you, you don't know what you're getting into."

The leader scowled. "What? Are you threatening me with a bunch of farmers and shopkeepers?" He peered at Hercules. "And a guy who can't even keep his shirt buttoned?"

"Uh-oh," Nikos muttered.

Hercules didn't lose the smile on his lips, but the smile faded from his eyes. "One last chance."

"Oh," the leader said, "this is boring. The hell with the talk."

With a great shout he charged, his men directly on his heels.

Immediately, a shower of arrows filled the air from the rooftops, most of them missing, the few that struck their targets doing so harmlessly. Rocks flew. Villagers braced themselves. The leader reached the center of the barrier and scrambled between the wheels.

Not fast enough, however.

Hercules reached down and grabbed his left arm, yanked him off his feet and into the wagon bed. As the others reached the wall and began to shove the carts and wagons apart with an ease born of practice—and carts and wagons that weren't all that heavy to begin with—Hercules hoisted the leader over his head, turned, and flung him effortlessly toward the well.

Meanwhile Nikos had brought one raider to his knees with a well-aimed blow to the shoulder, while the other raiders were busily bringing the villagers to their knees with the flat sides of their swords.

"Keep an eye out there," Hercules called to the archers. "There may be more."

"More?" It was the shadow man. "Double-doomed!"

Hercules jumped from the cart and grabbed the helmet of a passing raider. The raider ran on, Hercules smiled and sidearmed the helmet, whistling it through the air, catching the raider square on his naked skull.

A third man rammed a stunted club into Hercules' back. He gasped and stumbled forward, half turning as the raider thrust his sword toward his neck.

The sword never made it.

Nikos snapped it with his club, then transferred the momentum up and under the raider's chin, sending him off his feet and onto his back.

"Thanks," Hercules said.

Nikos looked at the fallen raider and said, "Wow."

The rest of the battle happened so quickly, Hercules barely had time to register the jaws struck, the bodies that flew, or bounced, or both, and the blows he himself took, most of them harmless and the others merely pesky.

Within a few minutes the attack part of the raid was over, and the villagers had won.

What raiders hadn't already been wounded or belted unconscious formed a loose protective circle around the well, facing outward, and already a half-dozen Markans lay at their feet; in the firelight their blood sank blackly into the ground. It was clear to Hercules that they believed they would easily be able to stave off any further village assault until the rest of their band arrived to rescue them.

He also knew there was little time left. The Markans were brave, but they just weren't warriors.

As another wave of villagers tried to break the raiders' defense, he turned back to the "wall," inspected it quickly, and discovered a fallen lance beneath one, caught under a wheel the largest, heaviest wagon.

"What are you doing?" Nikos asked.

An archer tried to pick the raiders off, and was picked off himself.

His scream was swallowed by the night.

Hercules tugged at the lance, cursed when it

39

wouldn't loosen easily, and grabbed hold of the wheel's thick spokes; he lifted, muscles swelling, eyes partially closed.

A young man rolled on the ground in agony, clutching a gash in his shoulder; another knelt before the raiders, his hands pressed tightly to his stomach.

The wagon protested loudly, creaking, then shrieking, then groaning as it rose, just enough for Hercules to nudge the lance aside with his foot. When he dropped the wagon and stepped back quickly, the axle split and the wagon collapsed.

"Sorry," he said, and picked up the lance, held it in both hands, and turned.

"There're too many," Nikos said, worried.

"Watch," was all Hercules offered as he advanced cautiously on the well.

Nikos waved the rest of his men into a charge.

The raiders braced themselves while their leader stood on the lip and snarled, his sword sweeping back and forth. He muttered something then, and Hercules suspected he knew what it was.

A moment later the man jumped from the well, his men forming a wall that pushed toward the carts, and the freedom beyond.

The villagers were knocked aside like high grass before a great wind.

Hercules charged as well, the lance held lengthwise in front of him.

He stopped abruptly and snapped his arms out, releasing the heavy weapon, which struck the front four raiders squarely across their chests, knocking them off their feet. He sprang over them to face their leader.

The raider didn't stop his charge or change direction. His sword lifted, and he swung his shield. Hercules blocked it with his left forearm, grunted at the impact, and ducked when the sword chopped at his head. Lashing out instantly with his right leg, his foot caught the man's knee and tumbled him face first into his men.

Within seconds the villagers had pounced, snatching weapons away, using whatever came to hand to pound the surviving raiders senseless.

When it over, and it was over quickly, there was another silence.

This one, however, was soon puncutated by the groans of the wounded, the pleas of the dying, and the muffled weeping of the women who had come to the site to tend to the fallen.

Hercules wasted no time.

He ordered the attackers doused with water to bring them around, then ordered three, including the leader, to be bound hand and foot. The others he ordered chained together at the wrist after stripping them of their armor.

"I don't get it," Nikos said, following as Hercules led the survivors toward the road.

"We're letting them go."

"What?"

"They'll go back to this Zorin and tell him what happened here. One man might be accused of cowardice, and lying to save his own skin. So might two. But these miserable . . ." He nodded in disgust at the seven strung out behind him. "These will be the truth."

"But what are they going to tell Zorin?" Nikos wiped his face and stared in surprise at the blood he saw on his palm. "He'll just bring his whole band back to get revenge, and we'll all be dead anyway."

"No," Hercules said.

He dragged the men to the road, grabbed the first in line by the throat, and said, "You heard?"

The man, bruised and cut over one eye, nodded fearfully.

Hercules nodded, and lowered his voice. "Then you tell him this, too, *friend*. You tell him this village has my protection, do you understand?"

The man nodded again, so hard his teeth clacked.

"Oh, yeah?" The second man, who seemed to have lost one ear, sneered. "So who the hell are you?"

Hercules stood in front of him, grabbed his shoulders, and yanked him so close their noses nearly touched.

"Hercules," he said tightly. "You tell this Zorin it's Hercules."

No one said a word.

Hercules stood aside and jerked a thumb. Immediately, the line began to move, stumbling weakly along the road, cursing, complaining, until they vanished into the night.

"You know," Nikos said after a few moments, "you're scary when you're mad."

Hercules looked at him. "Believe me, Nikos, you haven't seen me when I'm mad."

Slowly he returned to the square, and felt sick at what he saw. Too many had been injured, too many had died. It was evident that the tales about Zorin's raiders understated their brutality, if this is what only a handful of them could do.

No wonder there weren't any more of them out there; there didn't need to be.

"Nikos," he said when the innkeeper came up beside him, "do you have someone you trust to take over your inn for a few days?"

Startled, Nikos nodded. "But why?"

Hercules pointed to the remaining prisoners. "We're taking them on a trip."

"We are? Where?"

"King Arclin," he said. "We're taking them to King Arclin."

5

"You know," said Nikos, late the following afternoon, "I'm not really a fighter."

Hercules simply moved his head in an automatic nod. The innkeeper had been building up to this ever since they had left Markan, and he figured he had better let the man speak now, or he'd be at it all night and neither one of them would get a wink of sleep.

"Really. I'm not."

Hercules had borrowed an open, two-horse wagon from one of the merchants, and the three remaining raiders were now in back, tied, grumbling about the dust and the ruts and the lousy food service, of which, as a matter of fact, there hadn't been any. Generally behaving, that is to say, like prisoners who had no intention of giving their warders an easy time of it. Especially their leader, Theo—Theo the Mangler, he

44

called himself, for reasons Hercules decided he didn't want to know.

"I mean, the club is okay for what it does, you see. But that's not the real me."

Hercules, the reins easy in his hands, made several wordless but respectful noises.

"You see, the real me is more what you call your basic peace-loving man, you see what I mean? The club is only a symbol. The most I ever used it for was whacking a table now and then to keep the rowdies from tearing up the place. I never would have used it. I don't think I could."

"You were all right last night, pal," Theo the Mangler grumbled sourly. He struggled with his bonds a little, but more out of a sense of obligation than any real hope of breaking free. Thick rope tightly wound about a man's chest and ankles tended to do that to a prisoner.

Nikos looked over his shoulder. "Oh, well, that was different. I mean, you were trying to kill me, weren't you?"

"Damn straight."

"Well, there, you see? Self-defense. Any man can engage in self-defense without losing his peace-loving nature, you understand? Wouldn't be natural otherwise."

The Mangler shifted uncomfortably, trying to force more room between himself and his compatriots.

They would have moved, too, if they could have. They couldn't. The wagon was too small, barely wide enough for the three of them to stretch out their legs. If their knees bent a little. And they weren't too fussy about sudden cramps.

"What I see," the raider said, "is that peace-loving men are sheep, who don't deserve to have a life."

Nikos frowned. "Well, that's a matter for debate, don't you think?"

Theo growled.

"Exactly." Nikos grinned.

Exactly what? Hercules wondered, but didn't ask. If he asked, Nikos would probably tell him. And take his time about it, too.

As it was, they still had another day's travel ahead of them, and he wasn't all that sure the entire trip would be uneventful. Not that he didn't mind traveling; he did it all the time. It was, as a friend of his once said, part of his job description. What he did mind, however, were the horses. He seldom rode them. He walked everywhere it was possible to walk, riding only in emergencies, and even then he would have preferred that while riding he be unconscious.

He wasn't afraid of the beasts; he just didn't trust them very much. They had disturbing tendencies to stop short for no clear reason, and never mind the poor saps riding on their backs who, when the horses stopped short, generally weren't on their backs anymore.

He clucked softly. The two blacks shook their heads and pulled a little faster.

At least he didn't have to ride over mountains, or forge raging rivers, or cross rickety bridges over thousand-foot ravines. Most of the countryside had thus far been rolling pasture and meadowland, the forest having long since fallen away to the foothills in the hazy distance. A comfortable breeze kept the flies away, and its direction kept the dust from choking them. Even the road itself wasn't all that bad, what with ruts at a minimum and rocks pretty much all harvested for well walls, pasture boundaries, and such.

"Has it ever occurred to you," Theo snarled, "that Zorin is probably looking for us?"

"Good grief, no," Nikos said, twisting around now, one arm resting on the board that served as the driver's backrest. "He'll be too busy trying to figure out what he should do about Hercules."

The other raiders mumbled.

Theo scowled. "Come on. You think Zorin is afraid of Hercules?"

"If he's smart, he would be."

Theo laughed derisively. He glared at the others, and they laughed, too. "Zorin isn't afraid of anything, my friend. Not even the gods."

Nikos huffed. "That's because he hasn't met Hercules."

"Even then."

"Oh, I don't think so."

"My hat."

Nikos frowned. "What?"

Theo said, "My hat. I can't see. My bloody hat's fallen over my eyes."

Hercules couldn't help it; he looked. And it had. He looked back to the road that led them away from the setting sun and thought, I have fought against veritable armies; I have battled a couple of gods and more than my share of monsters; I have been bloodied and had some bones broken, I've been chained and whipped and nearly drowned, and come close to ending up in the Elysian Fields more than once . . . and this is where it all leads?

To a man who calls himself Theo the Mangler and complains about his stupid helmet? He should look in a stream sometime—those horns made him look like a sickly goat.

Nikos leaned over and straightened it.

"Thanks," said Theo.

"A peace-loving man," said the innkeeper, "always knows how to keep his customers happy." Then he turned to Hercules. "Really. I'm not a fighter."

"All right, Nikos, all right," he said wearily. "What's the point?"

"Ah. Well, you see, the point is, we're going to the king, right?"

"Right."

"Ha!" Theo said.

"Now, when we get there, the king will want to hear the whole story, right?"

"Right."

"Ha!" Theo said.

"And when he hears the whole story, he'll be upset because Zorin's back in his kingdom. Plying his trade, so to speak. The king, the gods love 'im, he'll have to send out part of his army—which isn't all that big in the first place, since we're such a small kingdom in the second place—to try to drive Zorin away again. Right?"

Hercules agreed, although it took him a moment.

Theo said, "You wish."

Nikos sighed. "And that means he'll want us—you and me, that is—to be a part of that army. On account of what we've already done. And I can't be, you see. I have a business to run. I'm not a professional fighter—"

"Got that in one." Theo sneered.

"—and I have a young son to take care of. Why, any one of Zorin's men would see through me in an instant, and then who would take care of Bestor? Who would keep him from living in the streets and becoming an urchin?"

49

"Nikos . . ." Hercules began.

"I'd probably have to carry a sword, too."

"Nikos."

"And wear armor and things. I hate armor. Have you ever had to wear armor, Hercules? It binds. The leather's not so bad, I guess, but to wear one of those breastplates? Forget it. I mean, you can barely breathe in the stuff."

"If you're a man," Theo said, "you can breathe."

"No," Nikos said, ignoring the raider, "I don't think I can do it."

Hercules had been afraid of this. The innkeeper's nerves had been twanging like the strings of a badly tuned lyre ever since the sun had been high. Now that they had to find a decent place to camp for the night, simply touching him on the shoulder would probably send him shrieking off the wagon and into the hills.

"Maybe you won't have to fight," Hercules said calmly.

Up ahead, he noticed a small stream near a stand of oak, not far off the road.

"I won't?"

"No, my friend, you won't. I'll see to it."

Nikos sagged in relief. "Oh."

"Besides," Theo scoffed from the back, "you'd be dead in an instant, one look at Zorin and his fire. Cowards are like that. They die easily."

He laughed.

His men laughed.

Nikos reached down into the gap beneath his legs, pulled out his club, turned, and whacked Theo none too lightly on his skull. "Peace-loving men," he said smugly in the abrupt silence, "don't have to take any crap from a man who can't keep his stupid horns on."

The fire was low and warm, the stars high and cold. Beyond the reach of the flames, the stream babbled softly. The horses had been unhitched and led away to be tethered in a rich grassy area, the raiders were still in the wagon bed, snoring, and Nikos had wrapped himself a furry cloak and was even now mumbling, "Not a fighter," in his sleep.

Hercules took the first watch.

He sat with his back against a half-buried boulder, a similar cloak borrowed from Nikos' pack around his own shoulders, listening to the night.

Listening for sounds that didn't belong.

He didn't expect Zorin, or any of his men, to try to rescue the raider trio. From all he had heard these past two days, the man would just as soon let them die. But King Arclin ought to be able to garner useful information from them; enough, perhaps, to better protect his people.

From all Nikos had told him, Arclin was a fairly content man. Others in his position might well cast a covetous eye on any or all of his neighbors. A kingdom this small, however, was not only easy to defend, it was easy to govern. And with a small population, most of it doing rather well, there was little threat of rebellion.

King Arclin was not as famous as, say, Midas, or other kings of renown, but even Hercules had heard of his vaunted army. Fierce. Veterans all. Canny about using their numbers to the greatest effect. And unwaveringly loyal to their sovereign.

It appeared to be the perfect situation.

So why, then, Hercules wondered, did he feel as if he were about to make a major mistake?

He yawned, and stretched.

He wasn't, he told himself as he shook his head sharply. This was no mistake, it was good sense. Give the king needed information, make sure he understood it was from the people at Markan, and the people of Markan would have a ruler in their debt.

Perfect sense.

He scowled briefly.

What you are is, you're tired, right?

Right.

You need a decent night's sleep, you know you're not going to get one because there's no way you'll be able to depend on the innkeeper to stay awake for more that five minutes, and so your brain is working overtime. Creating problems where there aren't any so you'll have something to do while you watch the fire, and the shadows.

While you listen to the gentle voice of the stream.

While you listen to the sound of a night bird gently fluttering its wings from one hunting ground to another.

The horses shied; one of them whickered quietly.

Night bird?

He listened more closely, then slowly, without making a sound, used the boulder to prop himself into a watchful half crouch, using the huge rock as his shield.

What night bird has wings that flap that loudly?

Theo the Mangler snorted in his sleep.

The horses shied again, this time more urgently.

Cautiously, Hercules peered over the rock, but could see nothing but the dark. The moon was gone, and the fading firelight didn't reach very far in any direction now. When he stared too long, things began to move out there where he knew nothing was.

He rubbed his eyes, checked again, and again saw nothing out of place.

When he turned back, all he could see was a lump that was the sleeping Nikos, and beyond that, the near side of the wagon, over which poked two metal-ribbon helms and a pair of dented horns.

He heard the wings again.

A signal? Men sneaking in through the grove? Ordinary bandits, or had he been wrong about Zorin?

He reckoned there was a good fifty feet between himself and the club Nikos had left on the driver's seat.

He listened.

He braced himself.

The wings stopped, and a slightly high voice complained, ''You know, Hercules, for a demigod, you're a hell of a hard man to find.''

6

Many miles' hard ride to the east were two mountains whose upper slopes had been scoured for aeons by the sword's edge of constant howling winds. Nothing grew there; everything that tried, died. The ground was bare rock and scattered boulders, and what little earth there was had been trampled into what felt like stone underfoot.

The peaks were jagged, slicing clouds and parting the wind.

During winter there was snow; the rest of the year there was no rain.

Animals from the fertile plain below seldom made the journey up, and birds never flew there; they took the long way around.

Between these nameless mountains was a narrow valley, so protected by them that it seemed another world entirely from the surrounding countryside. Lush grass, a stream that broke from the near vertical back slope to vanish into a pool midway along, a scattering of broad-crowned trees, and a temperature night and day that was preternaturally constant.

The only entrance was between two huge slabs of rock oddly marked by striations of white and dull red, the gap itself protected by a fifteen-foot gate of thick, unyielding wood banded in rust-pocked iron, with a brace inside made from three trunks lashed together. A quartet of sentries in fur and leather stood on a wood ledge above the gates, each with a bow and lance. A second quartet patrolled the grove of sycamore sixty yards away, down an easy slope that didn't stop until it reached the plain, nearly a mile away.

In the valley itself there were many lights from large fires, some in pits, some from torches, all reflecting off the polished stone of the north and south slopes. Midway along, near the south wall, a corral held nearly half a hundred horses; another beside it held cattle and oxen. Pigs and chickens roamed a fenced yard on the north side of the stream. There were no huts, only tents, but of these there were many.

Enough to hold a population of two hundred, maybe more.

There were no children.

There were no women.

The largest tent was at the valley's head, not far

from where the mountains rejoined in a solid wall of rock.

The tent was black, all of it, from the overhang at the entrance to the pennants that flew from poles poking through the top.

It was guarded by twenty men, none of whom were without battle scars of one sort or another, all of whom would have laid down their lives for their leader.

In the tent, at the rear, was a high-backed, throne-like chair raised two steps on a dais. Both chair and dais were covered with luxuriant fur that seemed alive in the shimmering light provided by the fire burning in a huge pit dug in the center of the hard-packed floor, and by lamps hanging from the tent poles.

From the chair, Zorin studied the last of seven men who had been dragged before him in chains this night.

The others had been carted away after only a few easy questions. Of the dozen men who remained inside—Zorin's inner council—not a one reacted to what screams they eventually heard.

The last man, stripped to the waist, his chest and back red with welts, couldn't look anywhere but at the ground. His arms were behind him, lashed around a short pole stripped of its bark; his hair hung damply over his face.

"You were lucky," Zorin told him kindly. "It's not all my men who find travel so swift and easy."

The man swayed, but didn't fall.

Some said Zorin's hair had been fashioned from the wings of a giant raven, a reference to its color and the way it swept upward when it reached his shoulders. Some said his beard had been fashioned from the raven's breast, a reference to its color and how thick and soft it looked.

No one ever asked what had happened to the raven.

"And you say it was, what, pretty much one man, a single man who beat you?"

The man shivered as if from the cold. Except the tent was hot, the pit's fire roaring with freshly added wood, its smoke billowing through a hole in the peaked roof.

"What?" Zorin leaned forward, cupping a hand around one ear. "I'm sorry, I didn't hear you."

"Y-yes," the man stuttered.

"And this man. His name is . . . what?"

"Her-Her-Hercules, my lord."

"I see."

Zorin leaned back, crossed one leg over the other at the knee, and looked toward his lieutenant standing below him. "Crisalt, is this true?"

If Zorin's color was born of the raven, the color of Crisalt's hair and mustache had been fashioned from the raven's blood.

"As far we can tell, my lord. That's what all of them told us anyway."

58

The prisoner who had once been a raider finally collapsed to his knees.

Zorin ignored him. "And this Hercules took three prisoners, is that right?"

"That's right. There was Theo, and . . . let's see . . ." Crisalt hesitated, closed one eye in concentration, and shrugged his apology. "I don't remember the others."

"It doesn't matter. They're dead anyway."

Crisalt agreed. "But Hercules is taking them to King Arclin."

Zorin's hand waved the point away. "Who cares?"

Crisalt agreed again.

Zorin considered the tips of his fingers for a few seconds, then rose and stepped down from the dais to stand over the prisoner. "And . . ." His voice rose slightly. "And Hercules told you to tell me that this village . . ." He paused, looked over his shoulder, snapped a finger.

"Markan," Crisalt told him.

"Yes, yes, Markan. That Markan is now under his protection, and I'm to keep my distance?"

After a long hesitation the prisoner nodded.

Zorin could see the blood drying on the man's back, could see the pattern of lashes a whip had laid across it. He crouched down and balanced on his toes, rocking slightly as he hooked a finger under the man's chin and forced his face up.

He smiled.

The prisoner shuddered.

"And what," Zorin asked softly, "do you think he meant by that, man?"

The prisoner tried to speak, but Zorin's finger held his mouth closed.

"A threat?" Zorin frowned, but kept his voice low. "What a shame." He lifted the face higher, straining the man's neck muscles. "Do you think he knows what happens to those who threaten Zorin?"

He couldn't tell if the man had suddenly been taken by a seizure or was only trying to shake his head.

It didn't matter.

He snapped his hand up so fast, not even Crisalt could tell exactly when the prisoner's neck snapped, or when, precisely, the flesh parted at the hollow of his throat.

Zorin watched the man topple to one side, stared at the body and blood in distaste for a moment, and stood. Slowly. Making sure the others saw how annoyed he was.

How angry he was.

How enraged he was.

"Crisalt."

"Sir!"

Zorin returned to the dais, but instead of taking his seat again, he walked around to the back. To a large iron chest wrapped in silver chains.

Red light glowed from cracks in the metal.

Crisalt joined him.

"Any word?" Zorin asked as he scratched thoughtfully through his beard.

"Not yet, no."

"What do you think?"

Crisalt was the only man in Zorin's army who dared speak his mind. He was also the only man who knew when to speak his mind, and when to keep his big mouth shut.

He grunted noncommittally.

"Good point." Zorin caressed one of the silver chains.

The chest seemed to vibrate.

"Tell me something, my friend."

The only sound in the tent was the voice of the fire.

Crisalt didn't move, didn't speak. When his leader spent valuable time staring at the chest instead of planning the next attack, there was bound to be trouble. It never failed.

"Why do you suppose a man who tends oxen would call himself Theo the Mangler?"

Well, hardly ever failed.

"Self-esteem," said Crisalt instantly.

"Really?"

"It was his first time, you know, my lord. He probably needed something to build up his courage."

"Ah." Zorin nodded his approval. "Not a bad idea."

"No, my lord."

"But he did fail, didn't he?"

"Yes, my lord."

"Which means he has to die, doesn't it, Crisalt?"

"Yes, my lord."

"So tell me, my friend . . . how do you kill someone who calls himself the Mangler?"

Crisalt was stumped. Zorin's expression gave nothing away, nor did his hand cease caressing the silver chain. Not that it was all that important. Theo the Idiot would be interrogated by the king, would escape the dungeon thanks to a few well-placed dinars here and there, would come hightailing it back to the valley, and would be bloody lucky Zorin didn't pull him apart personally, limb by limb, before anyone said, "Hello, Theo, where've you been?"

Several minutes passed.

Neither man said a word.

Shadows on the tent's back wall crawled like snakes toward the top.

"I will tell you something, old friend," Zorin said, in a voice Crisalt had never heard before.

"I'm listening."

Zorin turned his back on the chest. "If it hadn't been for those two thieves, I would probably be shaking in my boots right now."

Crisalt couldn't believe it.

Zorin tapped the man's sternum hard with a finger. "Hercules is no man to fool with, make no mistake about it. Never, never underestimate him, Crisalt. Never." A glance at the chest. "Even with the fire, he won't be easy to kill."

Crisalt did his best to keep his face a blank.

Then Zorin grinned. "But make no mistake about this, either, old friend. He will die. He *will* die."

7

Hercules sat heavily on the ground, one hand pressed to his chest to make sure his heart didn't get away. His lungs weren't working all that well, either, and it was all he could do not to pick the boulder up and smash it over the head of the man who stood before him, grinning like an idiot.

"Scared you, did I?"

"Go away," Hercules said.

"Can't. Have a message for you."

Hercules reached for the boulder, changed his mind, and sagged against it instead, hands limp on his thighs. "All right, all right. But"—he pointed sternly—"don't you ever do that again, you hear? You do and I'll pluck your bloody wings off. One by one."

Hermes, Messenger of the Gods, Master Thief, and

occasional all-around pain in the ass as far as Hercules was concerned, pouted. "That's no way to talk to an old friend, is it? I haven't seen you in absolutely ages." Lithe as a cat, he sat cross-legged on a patch of grass, jamming his caduceus into the ground beside him and causing its wings to flutter in agitation. The two snakes that coiled around the golden shaft only hissed resignedly; they were used to being ignored, and treated shabbily to boot. "Why, the last time I saw you was . . . when? Oh my goodness, I can't think how long ago it was. Do you remember? It'll come to me, though. Just give me a sec, I'll bring it back."

Hercules glanced over at Nikos, looked back at Hermes, and wondered if there could possibly be a family connection. He wouldn't have been surprised.

Hermes was, even for a god, of average height, a little on the skinny side, with almost blond hair that curled gently from under his winged cap. He was also prone to fussing when he wasn't sneaking around with messages or stealing things or inventing things—like the lyre. Which, just two years earlier, he had tried to improve by adding a copper gizmo, which, when struck by lightning, would make the lyre virtually scream. The problem was, as Hermes had been the first to admit, the lightning also fried the player. One-note songs, evidently, were not destined to survive, or be popular at weddings.

Still, Hercules decided, it was good to see him.

Unlike some other gods and demigods he could mention, Hermes was basically honest, reasonably fair, and could be counted on to do as he promised.

But he was also a sartorial failure.

Tonight, for example, he had opted to match his silver, winged cap with a puffy, silver kilt that barely reached to midthigh. That wouldn't have been so bad had it not been for the pearls on the kilt, whose design—resembling a bald man with one eye—probably had some significance other than its appearance suggested.

He wore no top, neither shirt nor vest.

Hermes was also proud of his physique. Such as it was. Which, Hercules thought, wasn't much.

"What," he said, interrupting the messenger's blathering, "do you want?"

"You know," Hermes said, adjusting his cap and patting the wings thereon to calm them, "I've decided this kilt thing is a bust." He tried futilely to tug the garment in question down around his knees. "My legs, you know, deserve better framing, don't you think?" He admired them, looked up in hopes that Hercules would admire them as well, saw that he wouldn't, and sighed. "What do you know, anyway?"

"Nothing," Hercules admitted, unable to stop a brief smile. "Not unless you tell me."

A stirring by the fire made Hercules put a finger to his lips.

Hermes nodded knowingly, adjusted his cap and kilt again, then stroked the wings on his sandals. He squinted into the middle distance, lips moving as he repeated the message to himself, then broke into a broad smile. "Got it."

"Fine."

Nikos snored, sputtered, and burrowed deeper under his cloak until only his nose was exposed.

Hermes cleared his throat and lay a hand on the flat of his chest.

"No," Hercules said hastily.

Hermes looked shocked. "No? What do you mean, no?"

"I mean, no singing."

Hermes *was* shocked. "What do you mean, no singing?"

Theo the Mangler shifted in the wagon, and his horns fell off.

"Look," Hercules said patiently, "I've had a long day, no sleep, little enough to eat, and I've a long day tomorrow. I've got three prisoners over there I have to take to King Arclin for interrogation, an innkeeper who isn't a fighter, and . . ." He cocked one eyebrow. "And a sneaking suspicion you already know all this."

Hermes acted insulted. "Me? How would I know?

I've been looking for you for practically months.''

"The message.''

Hermes cleared his throat.

Hercules glared.

Hermes pouted again. "You have no sense of culture, Hercules. No sense of the arts.''

"The message. Please.''

"Okay, but you aren't going to like it.''

Although Hermes was the messenger for all the gods, his primary missions generally came from Zeus.

Hercules hadn't spoken to his father in well over a year. Not since his wife and children had been killed by Hera, and Zeus hadn't done a thing to prevent the slaughter.

It was part of the curse of his destiny.

Source of his worst nightmares.

He gestured with one hand: *Go ahead, I'm ready, give it to me.*

Hermes sat straighter. "Some months ago, after many, many weeks of thought and preparation, a special gift was prepared for Zeus. A very special gift. A gift fit only for a god. A gift of such magnificence and radiance that only a god would appreciate its true value. A gift—''

Hercules leaned over and grabbed Hermes' knee.

"What? What?'' Hermes wanted to know.

"Spare me the embellishments, please?''

"What? But the embellishments are the best part.

It takes me forever to get them right. You have no idea, my dear, how right they have to be. Otherwise ... why, otherwise, your message might as well be written on a rock for every Nik and Nora to read.'' Indignant, Hermes yanked at the kilt's hem, and winced when he heard the distinct sound of cloth ripping.

''And I suppose I deserve those embellishments?''

''But of course!''

''And without them the message would say ... ?''

''Well, without them, to the untrained ear, it would say Hephaestos made a gift for Zeus, some jokers found a way inside the new forge, swiped it, and nobody's seen it since.''

Hercules opened his mouth, closed it, leaned back against the boulder, and stared at the stars.

Zorin's Fire.

The raider had said something about Zorin's Fire.

''This gift,'' he said.

''Magnificent,'' Hermes declared. His hands fluttered in the air in a vain attempt to describe it nonverbally; his sandal wings grew so excited, they lifted his feet off the ground and toppled him onto his back ... or would have done so had not the cap's wings counterbalanced the movement with frantic flapping of their own. The result was Hermes sitting in midair, rocking back and forth and looking well on his way to getting seasick, or airsick.

"What," Hercules said, "was the gift? Exactly."

Hermes grimaced an apology and worked first on getting himself back on the ground. Once done, he tugged on the kilt, fixed his cap, and said, "A sword."

I don't think I want to hear the rest of this, Hercules thought.

"A sword of fire."

I definitely don't want to hear any more of this.

"Not really of fire, of course, or no one but old Hephaestos could hold it. But fire can be summoned from it."

Hercules held up a palm to shut the messenger up.

"A very special sort of fire."

He held up the other palm.

"There is, according to Hephaestos, nothing in this world that can protect a man from it."

Hercules dropped his hands. "Swell."

"Hephaestos wants you to get it back."

"Wonderful."

"He says, if you do this for him, he'll make you a special sword all your own."

"Great. But I don't use swords."

"He thought of that. He said that if you don't want a sword, you can have a date with his wife."

"If I date Aphrodite, he'll kill me."

"He thought of that. He said if you don't want a date with his wife—and he won't be offended if you don't—he'll forge a special lining for those absolutely hideous armbands of yours. You'll be able knock a mountain down with one swing of one arm.''

Hercules examined the thick, woven leather that bound his arms from wrist to elbow. "Hideous?"

"Well, of course, Hercules. My dear, they're so déclassé, don't you know."

Hercules looked at him. "Déclassé?"

Hermes shrugged. "I don't know either. Some foreign word, I think. Macedonian or something. But it sounds right, don't you think? I mean, really, Hercules, you ought to do something about your wardrobe anyway, what with those . . ."

Hercules let him ramble on, not listening, nodding now and again, smiling weakly, while he thought about the proposal.

To do something that would benefit Zeus, who had let his family die so horribly, was out of the question.

Yet Hephaestos was a wonderful old sort, who could work positive magic with his hammer and anvil, forge and fire. Of all Hercules' brothers or half brothers, depending on who did the bragging, Hephaestos was very likely his favorite, with Hermes a close second. To turn him down would hurt the man deeply.

Yet by accepting, he would be helping Zeus.

In his haste to refuse the request, he almost cut Hermes off, then heard Nikos stirring again. Thinking

71

of Nikos reminded him of Bestor, and Lydia, and Dutricia . . . and the raiders.

The people who had died in Markan.

And those who had died elsewhere at the hands of Zorin's men.

He exhaled slowly, and loudly.

"Not to mention that shirt thing," Hermes continued, plucking at it in disgust. "I mean, that sort of yellowish whatever does complement your hair, I'll give it that much, but . . ." He shook his head and shuddered.

"I'll do it," Hercules told him.

Hermes' eyes widened in delight. "Now that's the first smart thing you've said all night." He fumbled with his kilt for a moment, and cursed. "Nuts. I forgot pockets. No matter. I know the address by heart."

"What address?"

"Of a perfectly divine, so to speak, tailor. He'll have you fixed up in no time, believe me. Why—"

"No," Hercules said. He smiled to soften the refusal's sting. "Thanks, but no. I will try to get Hephaestos' sword back, though." The smile faded quickly. "I can't let it remain here. It belongs with . . ." He couldn't say it, and was grateful when Hermes nodded his understanding. "You will take a message to Hephaestos, then?"

"Oh, no, really?" Hermes' voice rose. "Do you have any idea how hot it is there? And it isn't even

Etna, for crying out loud. It's his new summer place, some mountain I never heard of. The Other Side should be so hot."

Hercules laughed quietly. "You can't refuse the message."

"I know."

"So you'll tell him?"

Hermes nodded reluctantly. "But, dammit, it'll have more embellishments than one of Aphrodite's gowns, I can tell you."

"Knock yourself out," Hercules said.

Hermes giggled, then laughed, and he and Hercules spent most of the next hour trading gossip, complaining about gods who acted as if they were, well, gods, and wondering, rather somberly, what the world was coming to when a couple of ordinary thieves could sneak into a god's lair and steal a piece of his soul.

When they were done, Hermes snapped orders at his wings, yanked the caduceus out of the ground, and hovered over the boulder. "I'll see you soon," he promised.

"Good," Hercules answered. "I'd like that."

As Hermes rose into the night, he added, "And I'll bring you a sample of that cloth. I mean, really, Hercules, yellow? Come on, it's not you."

Maybe it wasn't, he thought; but if the alternative was a silver kilt, he'd stick to the yellow.

To stretch his legs, then, he walked over to the

wagon to make sure the raiders were still bound. Satisfied they weren't about to get loose, he reached down, grabbed Theo's horned hat, and plopped it on the man's head, grinning when the Mangler grumbled in his sleep.

Nikos was practically buried by his cloak, only his prominent nose poking out.

The horses were fine, the night was fine, and as he settled back against his rock, he wished he were fine as well. Seeing Hermes again had brought back a lot of memories, not all of them bad, and it made him sad to realize that the feud with his father had substantially cut down on visitations from the Olympian side of the family.

That, in turn, made him angrier than ever at Zeus, his father.

Which, in turn, made him angry at himself for being angry.

And that cast him into a deep and troubled sleep.

When he awoke, his temper was short.

He opened his eyes shortly after sunrise, and it didn't help his temper at all when a large man with a lance in his hands and a plated helmet on his head pointed the weapon at him and said gruffly, "On your feet, boy. The king wants to see you."

8

Not having been called "boy" since childhood, Hercules reacted badly to the order. He grabbed the business end of the lance, used it and the soldier's surprise to yank himself to his feet, and was about to teach the man some manners when Nikos hustled over, waving his arms and explaining just who the soldier had on the other side of his weapon.

After a long moment's consideration, the soldier smiled.

Hercules smiled.

The soldier apologized and suggested that he would be extremely grateful if he could have his lance back. In one piece, thank you, please, and so sorry for the trouble, he was only following orders, and in this day and age, what with Zorin's raiders and all, a trooper can't be too careful.

Hercules told him it was all right, and anyway, he was always a little grumpy on first waking up.

When the soldier nodded his thanks and marched off to join a dozen others milling around the wagon and its prisoners, Hercules beckoned Nikos to his side.

"What's going on?"

"King Arclin," said the innkeeper breathlessly. "He heard we were on our way and sent an escort."

"He did."

"Yes." Nikos beamed with excitement. "A king's escort. Imagine that. I can't wait to tell Bestor and Lydia about this. This is going to make business at the Bull and Bullock boom, I can tell you."

Hercules, for his part, couldn't wait to find out just how the king had found out about this prisoner escort, but he said nothing just yet. He was hungry, for one thing, and for another, he was still half-asleep. So he accepted a measly ration from one of the soldiers, took his place on the wagon, and allowed another soldier to do all the driving.

Nikos, riding the driver's horse, was too ecstatic to do anything but babble.

Like a child, Hercules thought fondly, and despite the inordinate speed with which the escort took to the road, he managed to doze most of the way, noting only that Theo the Mangler was, for a change, quiet.

The morning passed in a blur of fields, shrubs, and

76

distant woodland. They passed few other travelers, but those they did pass always made way for the soldiers, greeting them with cheerful waves and calls of encouragement.

Nikos, meanwhile, quickly discovered the dubious wonders of riding horseback; specifically, the way the horse's spine regularly and not always rhythmically connected with the rump and spine of the rider. He did not complain, however. He smiled painfully, but bravely, at Hercules once in a while and kept his chin, and his nose, up.

They did not stop at midday, save for a minute or two at a stream to water the horses.

Hercules, his head throbbing from the speed at which the wagon took the road, discovering a marvel of new ruts and rocks along the way, glanced back to be sure the prisoners were still alive, not to mention still in the wagon. They were, it turned out, both of these things, although they jounced and bounced in such a way that he wondered if their heads were still attached to their necks.

Oddly enough, Theo, despite the discomfort, looked absolutely terrified, and only a stern whack on the head stopped his struggles to escape.

Curious, Hercules thought. He hadn't thought the king had such a formidable reputation; certainly not among those who rode with Zorin. He was impressed. Yet all attempts to speak with the raider were met with sullen grunts, and a handful of glances that suggested he mind his own business.

An hour later the escort leader swerved off the main road onto a wider, better-maintained one. It led across a broad plain directly toward a low, flat-topped rise in the middle distance and, it seemed from here, continued straight up the near slope. Huts began to appear along the roadside, and the escort was forced to slow as pedestrian traffic, mostly traders and merchants, began to grow.

Far to the left was a mountain range, clouded by a haze that almost concealed the barren upper slopes.

Finally Hercules could stand the thumping no longer and, with thanks to the driver, jumped to the ground. His legs wobbled a little from inaction, but his stomach and head calmed almost instantly. The prisoner escort was slow enough now that it was easy to keep up.

Nikos soon joined him. On foot.

"Another story to tell Bestor?" Hercules said, swerving to walk behind the wagon.

The innkeeper massaged his rump gingerly with both hands. "I don't think so. Those beasts ought to be outlawed. Do you know that thing tried to bite me? Ye gods, what teeth!" He slapped at his slightly bowed knees and groaned theatrically. "I feel like I've been strapped to a barrel and rolled from the top of Olympus."

Ahead they could hear the escort leader snarling at people to get out of his way.

The prisoners kept their heads down, although Hercules couldn't help but notice that once in a while Theo glanced in his direction.

"Wow," Nikos exclaimed when another hour had passed. "Will you look at that?"

"At what?"

Nikos pointed at the rise. "I was here once, you know. Quite a long time ago. I decided it would be fun to pay my taxes in person, just so I could see where the king lived." He grimaced. "Not that it was fun to pay the taxes, of course. The trip probably cost me more than I actually paid in tax money. But it was interesting. They actually thanked me when they took my money. Now it's all changed. Wow."

Hercules wasn't sure what the man meant.

The rise was quite long from east to west and, according to Nikos, easily that same distance from north to south. A small community, a veritable new city, was in the process of expanding around the base, permanent and temporary buildings of both stone and wood; yet there was nothing at all on the grassy slope.

On top was what appeared to be a single structure, of massively blocked gray stone and granite; the west end sprouted what he figured would eventually become a corner tower, and elaborate scaffolding had already been erected at the other corner he could see. When it was finished, it would be a truly impressive palace.

"It's bigger," Nikos said in awe. He tapped Hercules' arm. "Much bigger."

"How much bigger?"

"A lot."

Hercules nodded.

"It wasn't that way in the old days," Nikos finished.

There were fewer breaks along the shoulders now. Merchant stands, temporary lodgings, food stalls, money changers, the beginnings of alleys and streets. The road itself had been sealed with rounded paving stones, making the horses' hooves sound like whip cracks and causing the wagon to bounce and sway even more. Although the number of people wasn't large, the way still seemed crowded, and Hercules moved closer to the wagon.

Theo the Mangler glanced at him again, but did nothing more than scowl menacingly when Hercules raised an eyebrow in silent question.

"The old king, now, he had a really simple place," Nikos explained with a hint of nostalgia. He waved a hand at the palace ahead. "Nothing really fancy, you know? A couple of rooms, a courtyard, a place for parties, things like that. And the dungeons, of course.

He didn't want the people to think he was out of touch with their needs."

Hercules looked at him.

Nikos shrugged. "I don't know what he meant, either. He was a king. Kings talk funny sometimes."

The closer they drew to the rise, the more detail they could see in the new palace walls, mainly that there were no windows, no archer slits, no gaps at all.

Not a palace, Hercules thought; a fortress.

I think I don't like this.

"Amazing," Nikos said, his tone indicating that he wasn't sure whether he liked the new look or not.

Hercules slowed to allow the soldiers and wagon to pull ahead. "You said the old king."

"Sure. King Arclin the First. King Arclin the Second is his son."

The cluster of buildings came to an abrupt end, as if an invisible wall had been reached. Two hundred yards of open ground surrounded the king's rise, and the road did not continue on to the top, as Hercules had thought.

The road ended at the base; from there to the top were broad marble steps leading to a gap in the palace wall. Colorful pennants flew from the top. He could see guards stationed around the base. There were also long and low wood structures where the slope ended at the top, but he couldn't figure out what they were.

Nikos pointed at the way up. "One hundred"—a

frown, and one eye closed in thought—"and thirty-two steps." A grin now, proud. "I counted them as I went up."

"You must have been exhausted."

"Nah. I was younger then. And"—he scowled at his feet—"my legs were straight."

Hercules smiled briefly. "Nothing fancy here," he said, frowning as he scanned the blank wall.

"New king, new ideas."

The escort dismounted at the base of the steps, and as they hustled the prisoners out of the wagon, Hercules noticed that no one had followed them from the new city. That puzzled him. In other places, even those ruled by the worst tyrants, there are always crowds near the gates—beggars, petitioners, con men, hawkers, supplicants, mercenaries looking for work, thieves, and simple travelers.

This arrangement was strange.

A horn blew a single commanding note.

The soldiers immediately arranged themselves in two straight lines extending from the bottom step. The prisoners were forced to kneel, facing the steps.

Hercules and Nikos stood to one side at a silent order from the leader.

"There's something I forgot to tell you about King Arclin," Nikos whispered nervously.

A small figure in white appeared at the gate. Behind it stood two others holding long gold poles topped with blue-and-yellow plumes. To either side were clusters of men and women in clothing those in the new city would probably kill for, given half a chance.

"What's that?"

The figure descended slowly.

The horn blew.

The soldiers stiffened to attention.

Theo glanced back at Hercules; his arrogance was gone.

"Well . . . I don't want to be disrespectful, you know, but I don't want you to get in trouble either."

The horn blew, not very well; in fact, it wavered a little, and missed a couple of grace notes.

The figure was midway down the steps.

"So tell me," Hercules said from the corner of his mouth.

"Well . . ."

Hercules looked at the figure, blinked, and said, "Never mind, I think I've got it."

The king wore a flowing white robe, elaborately embroidered with broad gold and silver bands at the hem and around the edges of the flowing sleeves. Around his neck he wore a jeweled medallion in the shape of a multipointed star; on his wrists were copper and gold bracelets studded with jewels; on his feet he wore gold-tasseled sandals that seemed determined to catch themselves on the gown's hem; and on his head he wore a small but impressively jeweled crown.

He seemed young, with dark brown hair cropped short and slightly curled above his nape. His eyes were a startling cold blue, and he was lean and angled, and probably even younger than he looked.

He was also the shortest king Hercules had ever seen in his life.

9

That's him? Hercules thought in amazement; that's the king everyone's talking about? My gods, how do people keep from giggling?

"Willpower," Nikos whispered.

Hercules stifled a laugh, sobered immediately, and watched as the king halted on the third step, clasped his hands in front of him, and said, "Captain of the Guard?"

The escort leader stepped forward; even on level ground, he wasn't much shorter than the king on the third step.

"Do you have the prisoners?"

"Aye, sire. They appear before you now in disgrace and humiliation."

The king looked down his pudgy nose at the kneeling raiders. "That one has horns, Captain."

"Yes, sire."

"I don't like horns."

The captain instantly reached out and slapped Theo's hat from his head.

"Thank you."

"Your wish, sire."

"And the man who captured them?"

The captain pointed. "Hercules, sire, and a man called Nikos of Markan."

"Bring them to me."

The captain gestured.

Hercules didn't move, and grabbed Nikos' arm to keep him at his side.

A moment passed.

"Captain, are they moving?"

The captain gestured again, a little frantically this time. "Uh, no, sire, they're not."

Nikos hissed a warning, but Hercules held his place.

"Are they dead, Captain?"

The captain's eyes widened as he tried to stare Hercules into moving, and the import of his gesture changed from *you're going to get us killed* to *are you out of your bloody mind?*

Another second passed before Hercules stepped into the road, practically dragging Nikos behind him until they stopped just behind the raiders.

"My apologies," Hercules said. "My friend and I

86

aren't used to traveling so far, so fast.'' He smiled. Quickly. ''We're a little stiff.''

Nikos nodded so hard Hercules had to stop him before he made them both dizzy.

The king finally deigned to meet Hercules' gaze. ''I am pleased that such a famous individual would help one of our little communities. It does us great honor.''

''It's nothing,'' Hercules replied modestly.

''Oh, but no, it *is* something,'' the king insisted, his smile wide, his eyes nearly closing. ''These scum''—and he nodded to the prisoners—''have caused us so much trouble, you just don't know. That you were able to defeat them is a wonder. A veritable wonder.''

''You're too kind,'' Hercules replied. Modestly.

King Arclin preened, pudgy hands drifting over the folds of his royal gown. ''Yes, well, I do try, you know. I do try.'' A gesture caused the captain to snap an order, which, in turn, caused his men to grab the prisoners, yank them to their feet, and haul them up the steps toward the palace. The captain remained at his sovereign's side, but one step below so the king still managed a full inch's advantage.

Hercules saw that he sweated a little.

Arclin reached into one sleeve and fumbled around a bit before pulling out a small sack. He bounced it on his hand so that all within hearing would know there was money inside, and tossed it to Hercules.

Hercules snatched it, handed it to Nikos, and said, "Very generous. Markan will be pleased."

The king waved the gratitude away with a languid gesture. "It is only a cap on today's wonderful news, Hercules."

"Really?"

"Oh, yes." Another gesture, this one over his shoulder. "The small community of Drethic has decided to embrace our protection against the vile incursions of the vile Zorin." He grinned. "Along with our other modest political and geographical gains lately, my mapmakers are working overtime. I think two of them are going blind."

The captain guffawed for exactly three seconds.

Nikos chuckled weakly, but frowned a lot.

Hercules merely smiled his not terribly sincere congratulations, knowing as he did that Drethic was no small community, and the last he had heard, was definitely not within this kingdom's boundaries. Still, it wouldn't be the first time a border town had switched its allegiance from one king to another. Providing safety for his citizens was one of a ruler's primary obligations.

That, however, wasn't what bothered him.

It was the implication that Drethic wasn't the only town that had sought Arclin's protection.

The king made a gesture.

The captain made a gesture.

The horn blew a single note, clear and strong.

"Ah," Arclin said regretfully, "duty calls, I'm afraid. Thank you ever so much, Hercules and Nikos. You're always welcome at my table."

He turned, and Nikos stepped forward before Hercules could stop him.

"Sire?"

The king looked back, unpleasantly surprised. "Yes?"

The captain gestured and mugged frantically behind the king's back.

"Sire . . ." Nikos didn't know whether to stand or kneel, bow or genuflect, and so froze in a half crouch that made him look as if he had stomach cramps. "Sire, the raiders threatened to return, with Zorin himself, even though our friend Hercules warned him we are now under his protection. We . . . Zorin's Fire . . . we don't . . . I mean, Hercules has so many places to . . . I mean . . ."

He stammered into silence.

The horn blew a flourish.

The king gestured.

The captain gestured.

The horn shut up.

"My good man," the king said flatly, "Hercules is a busy man, as you have said. Markan is under my protection now, and you may tell your little people that they have nothing to fear from Zorin's Fire." He glared. "I will see to that."

Nikos nodded. "Yes, Your Majesty, thank you, Your Majesty, you're very kind, Your Majesty."

"Yes," Arclin said. "I am, aren't I?"

In as regal a fashion as he could manage without tripping over his robe, he ascended the steps toward his palace.

The captain, meanwhile, raced down the steps, whispered, "If you know what's good for you, you'll be out of here before sunset," to Hercules, raced back up the steps, and gestured just in time to get the horn going again before the king reached the unfinished gates.

Nikos moaned.

"What?" Hercules said.

"I can't straighten up."

Hercules rolled his eyes at the gods who gave him such powerful friends, helped Nikos stand, then looked up at the palace while the innkeeper tried not to fall over.

"Are we in trouble, Hercules?"

Hercules thought for a moment before he nodded.

"Why? What did we do?"

"Nothing." He turned toward the new city. "It's just that your good king knows something. And he thinks I know it, too."

"And do you?"

Another pause before: "Yes, I think I do."

"Is it that bad?"

"Bad enough, my friend, that if we don't do as the captain says, there's a chance we'll be dead by morning."

The problem with leaving town in a hurry, Hercules knew as he and Nikos left town in a hurry, is that walking wasn't nearly as efficient as a good horse would have been.

Still, they were able to make decent time once he was able to convince the innkeeper that testing every roadside meal stand for something he could use at the Bull and Bullock was not, under the circumstances, the best of ideas.

Dead with a full stomach was still dead. The only difference was, you didn't burp when you were done.

"But I don't get it," the innkeeper complained once they had left the last of the new city behind. "Why would King Arclin want us killed?"

"Not you, me."

"But I'm with you."

Hercules couldn't argue.

The sun had already begun its downward slide, the sky darkening, shadows filling the few trees scattered across the broad plain. A large flock of birds wheeled northward, the air filled with calls and cries. A rider galloped past them, heading toward the city.

No one passed them in the other direction.

"I can't die, you know," Nikos insisted quietly. "My son. I can't die."

"You won't," Hercules told him.

"But you said—"

"I said he probably wants us dead, and that's true. But that doesn't mean we'll die, my friend. At least not without a fight."

"Oh," Nikos said, "that makes me feel so much better."

Hercules laughed. "Okay, okay. Here's what I think's going on."

"Maybe you shouldn't tell me," Nikos interrupted apologetically. "What I don't know maybe won't hurt me."

"Maybe."

"Of course, like you said, I'm with you. And they would naturally think that, since we're kind of but not really partners, you'll tell me everything."

"Probably."

"Which means . . ." Nikos shuddered. "I don't live right, you know? I'm an innkeeper, not a fighter."

"Yes," Hercules said. "But for an innkeeper, you're a pretty good fighter anyway."

Nikos beamed.

Hercules checked behind them to be sure there were no riders on their trail. Then he explained.

For a small kingdom, and an even smaller king, there was, it seemed, an awful lot of construction going on at the palace. While the old king might have been content with what he had, it didn't appear to Hercules as if the new king was following in his father's footsteps. Hercules had seen the partial construction of one tower, which undoubtedly meant there would be at least three more. Without having been inside, he reckoned King Arclin II wasn't going to be satisfied with a couple of bedrooms, a great hall, a throne room, and a few meeting rooms. This palace looked to be striving for something usually found only around Athens, Corinth, or Sparta.

"The man has taste," Nikos suggested.

Hercules pictured the gold-tasseled sandals, and shook his head.

And with all due respect, he continued, he sincerely doubted that, as good as the king's army was, it was in any way so wondrous and marvelous that it would be able to protect the entire kingdom, especially since Arclin was adding new towns to his holdings somewhat frequently.

New towns did not come alone.

There was all the land that connected them, and Arclin didn't seem at all concerned that the rulers who owned those lands were probably more than a little annoyed.

Sooner or later one of them was going to step in. If it hadn't already happened.

"The army," Nikos reminded him.

The army, Hercules reminded him in turn, was small. He doubted it would be able to hold off much larger units from much larger, wealthier kingdoms whose leaders were probably royally pissed.

"But he's been able to stop Zorin, hasn't he?"

They reached the crossroads just as the sun sank below the horizon. Although dusk still provided some light, it was not enough for their needs. Hercules steered them to the left, back toward Markan. It was the obvious route to take should there be pursuers, but he had no knowledge of the terrain elsewhere, and this was no time to learn.

Nikos had been puffing for quite some time, and now added a touch of panting.

Nevertheless Hercules pressed on.

Of course, all his suspicions could be wasted. It might well be that Arclin was just a short king with tall ambitions. Whatever the hell that meant. Yet Hercules was determined not to take any chances. At least not until he was able to straighten out what he had gotten himself into this time.

A habit, he realized sourly, he had grown much too used to for his own peace of mind, and for keeping all his body parts where they belonged.

First, he had to make sure the king's men didn't

kill him and Nikos. Assuming they were going to try. Assuming Arclin suspected that Hercules suspected that not all was well and proper around here these days.

Then he had to figure out how he was going to keep his promise to Hephaestos, and recover the stolen sword. Assuming the stolen sword was recoverable. Assuming the stolen sword wasn't Zorin's Fire.

He snorted.

Well, of course it was. Any idiot could figure that one out. How else could Zorin be so successful, so quickly?

But if the stolen sword actually was Zorin's Fire, then why was Zorin content just to raid towns and villages now and then? Why didn't he aim for a larger prize, like Athens or . . . ?

With a grunt he stopped, and Nikos bumped into him, rebounded, and stared.

"Why," Hercules asked, "hasn't Zorin tried to take this kingdom as his own?"

Nikos stared.

"Why hasn't Zorin run amok around here? He certainly has the power to do it."

Nikos stared.

"How has King Arclin been able to stop Zorin, when Zorin has this powerful weapon? With his army? That army?"

Nikos stared.

"And what in blazes are you staring at, Nikos?"

Nikos interrupted his staring long enough to point tremulously over Hercules' shoulder.

Hercules turned, sighed, and said, "Now what?"

And Hermes, hovering about four feet off the ground, answered, "If you know so much, dear brother, why don't you stop asking so many questions and go get the thing before Hephaestos blows his top?" The messenger shuddered dramatically. "Literally."

"If I knew where it was," Hercules said testily.

"Well, that's why I'm back."

"You know where it is?"

"Yes." Hermes shuddered again. "But that's not all."

"What are you talking about?"

Three pairs of wings fluttered in agitation as Hermes smiled wanly and muttered, "Boy, you're not going to like this one."

10

Realizing that standing in the middle of the road with a winged god, even if it was nearly full dark, would probably draw some unwanted attention, Hercules hushed his brother with a gesture and suggested they head for the grove of oak he had spotted some hundred yards distant.

Hermes flew off without argument.

Nikos said he didn't think he could take any more wonders today, and would Hercules mind if maybe he just headed on home by himself?

Hercules did mind.

With a firm hand he guided the innkeeper across the plain to the grove, in the center of which they found Hermes, a warm fire already burning in a shallow pit and a large plucked bird turning slowly on a spit.

97

"I figured you were hungry," he explained, tossing a pinch of herbs over the roasting fowl.

"Thanks," Hercules answered as his stomach growled. "We are."

Nikos couldn't help himself: "How did you do that so fast?"

"God stuff," Hermes answered.

Nikos sniffed the air and sighed approval. "It smells wonderful."

"Thank you." A cocked eyebrow at Hercules. "At least someone around here appreciates me."

"Don't start," Hercules warned as he sat on the grass. "I'm not in the mood."

"It's not going to get any better," the messenger replied. He had abandoned the silver kilt for a long green tunic that reached his knees and was belted around the waist in basic black. From a small pouch on the belt he pulled three plates, passed them out, and used the hissing caduceus to slice pieces from the spitted bird.

Nikos blinked. "How did you do that? There's no blade."

"More god stuff," Hermes answered. "I like your cloak, by the way. Make it yourself?"

Nikos drew the fur cloak around his shoulders. "Actually, Lydia made it. She's very good at things like that." His voice softened. "It's only been a couple of days, you know, but I miss her already."

Hercules ate silently, wondering why he never thought of bringing a pack with him. The night air had chilled considerably, and although the fire was warm, he couldn't help feeling a chill on the back of his neck.

He suspected, however, that it had nothing to do with the temperature.

Once they declared themselves satisfied, Hermes smiled at Nikos and suggested that the innkeeper might want to catch a good night's sleep.

"Not tired," Nikos said. "This is too exciting."

"Oh, I don't know." The caduceus passed over the man's head. "You look exhausted to me."

Seconds later Nikos was on his back, a mound of leaves for a pillow, snoring softly.

"A good man," the god said.

"He is," Hercules agreed. "A very good man, who doesn't deserve any of this."

An owl questioned in the dark, and was answered by the bark of something passing the grove.

"Zorin's Fire," Hercules said at last. "It's the sword, isn't it? Hephaestos' stolen sword."

Hermes nodded. "I figured you would figure that out soon enough."

"But you said there's more."

"I did."

"And I wouldn't like it."

"You won't."

Hercules poked a stick at the fire, sending sparks spinning above their heads. "Do I have to guess?"

"Only if you want to." Hermes tried to smile. "It'd be more fun, actually. Heavy news on a heavy stomach is bad for your constitution."

"My constitution," Hercules said in a near growl, "is fine."

"Yes. I suppose it would be." Hermes settled himself across the pit, his face rippling with the reflection of the flames. "The way he told it to me, Hephaestos was out shopping or something with Aphrodite, see, when a band of thieves discovered his new home. You know, the summer one I told you about? They also found the sword, swiped it, and brought it back to Zorin." He sniffed. "Well, two of them did, anyway. The others were caught by Hephaestos' men and . . ." He made a face. "Well, let's just say Hephaestos won't need to look for fuel for a while."

Hercules didn't ask. He would have, but he didn't think his stomach could take it. His imagination had already done most of the work, and it raised goose-flesh along his arms.

"Anyway, these two gave the Fire to Zorin. Which you already know. What you don't know is what Hephaestos told me when I told him what you told me to tell him." He inhaled slowly. "He told me to tell you that if he doesn't have his sword back in four days, he's going to blow his top."

Hercules didn't have to ask about that one, either. He had already seen a handful of examples of what happened when Hephaestos blew his top. Mountains tended to disintegrate, lava tended to flow, and Hades tended to have a whole lot more people to deal with that he hadn't counted on during the normal course of collecting the spirits of the dead.

"Which top?" he asked.

"You know the mountains just north of King Arclin's new palace?"

Hercules' eyes widened. "What? You mean he's under one of those?"

Hermes nodded.

"But . . . but if he . . ." Hercules slapped his imagination a good one before it could complete the sequence of images it was bent on conjuring. "But how can I find Zorin, get the sword, and get it back to Hephaestos in four days?"

"Oh, that's easy. Have you seen those mountains up close?"

Hercules shook his head.

"There's a heavily guarded valley between them. Zorin's army camps there."

Hercules leaned away and stared at his half brother, leaned closer, and said, "If . . ." He shook his head, closed his eyes, opened his eyes, and said, "If Hephaestos is right next to the camp, why doesn't he get the sword himself?"

"I asked him that."

"And he said?"

"He said to remind you about the day of the pilgrims."

Hercules usually enjoyed visiting Hephaestos' forge. He wasn't all that thrilled about the constant heat, and the casual way Hephaestos handled a hammer and the fire made him nervous. But there was no doubt that the god was an artist. There was nothing he couldn't create out of iron and fire; and what he created, while not always magical, was always beautiful, always perfect.

One afternoon, Aphrodite had joined them, suggesting they come to the surface with her to enjoy the lovely spring day and get away from work for a while. Although Hephaestos, as was his manner, grumbled and complained and balked, there was nothing he wouldn't do for his wife. When they arrived, a group of pilgrims happened to pass, and while they were taken by the exquisite beauty of Hephaestos' wife, they were, to a man, terrified by Hephaestos himself.

It was the artisan god's curse that he was not only lame, he was ugly as well.

Hercules had never really noticed it; his half brother was, after all, his brother. In punishment for a past sin, Aphrodite had been given to Hephaestos as a wife, and ironically, they had turned out to be more devoted to each other than any other couple Hercules had ever known.

But the reaction of the pilgrims had hurt the virtuoso blacksmith deeply, so much so that he had vowed never to return to the land of Man again.

"If I did," he had said, "and even one of them laughs, I'd have to kill them all."

He hadn't been kidding.

And there was no doubt that Zorin's warriors were not the type to be sensitive to a man's feelings.

Or a god's.

"Great," Hercules muttered. "Oh . . . great."

Hephaestos comes out, someone laughs, and he blows everything up; Hephaestos doesn't come out, he doesn't get his sword back, and he blows everything up.

"Great. Just . . . great."

On the one hand, at least it won't take four days to reach the raider valley; on the other, Hercules was hardly the type to blend in with such a band. For one thing, he wasn't dressed for it. It wouldn't take them long to spot him, and despite his strength and agility, taking on an entire army was not a pleasant prospect.

He was a son of Zeus, but he definitely wasn't immortal.

"I hate quandaries," Hermes said blandly, "don't you?"

Hercules stared at the flames, at the images that flowed within them, letting his mind's eye trace paths only he could see. None of them seemed to lead to success.

What might have been a smile pulled at the corner of his mouth.

Maybe . . .

Sparks rose silently. A twig snapped almost noiselessly.

Without lifting his head, he looked up at Hermes. "I need to get into that palace."

"What?"

"I need to get arrested."

Hermes opened his mouth to ask the obvious question, but immediately closed it when the obvious answer occurred to him.

"It's dangerous," he said.

"So's a volcano."

"You could be killed outright."

"Maybe not."

"That shrimp of a king already knows what you look like. You're not going to fool him."

"I don't have to fool him, just a couple of guards. Just long enough for me to break those men out and have them lead me into the camp."

"What makes you think they'll do it?"

Hercules made a fist, and smiled without amusement.

Hermes shrugged one shoulder. "It could work. But how will you get into—" He stopped. He stared. He grabbed the caduceus, when it made a desperate attempt to fly away. "No. Absolutely not."

"Why not?"

"*Carry* you? Carry *you*? Are you out of your little demigod mind?"

The caduceus made another break for it, but Hermes was too quick.

Hercules laughed silently. "It's not that far, don't get so excited. Short hops so we can get there while it's still dark. Up and over the wall, and leave the rest to me."

Hermes shook his head. "Get serious, Hercules. I carry messages, not people. It's impossible. I'm sorry, but—" He frowned and looked off into the dark. "Did you hear that?"

"It's got to work, Hermes. It's the only way."

"Hush." The messenger rose into the air, hovered for a moment as he frowned, and suddenly darted away.

Hercules scowled, and jabbed the stick angrily at the fire. All right, so it wasn't the most brilliant plan in the world. All right, so maybe it was fundamentally flawed. But it was either that or have this part of the world buried in fire and ash, and its people nothing more than a memory.

His memory.

Which he would have to live with for the rest of his life.

Well, if Hermes wouldn't help him, he would have to do it himself.

He stood, looked fondly at the sleeping Nikos, and hoped that a good easy run would get him close enough to King Arclin's city before dawn. After that, he'd have to—

He jumped when something landed hard in the dark beyond the fire, yelped in pain, and yelped again when something smacked it.

"Hercules."

It was Hermes.

"Hercules, come here."

Cautiously Hercules walked around the pit, fingers flexing, peering into the far reaches of the firelight. He stopped when he saw his brother hovering over a bundle on the ground.

"I hope you're happy," Hermes complained. "I think I've strained my back."

The bundle groaned and shifted.

When it sat up, Hercules didn't know what to say, and so said, "Hello, Theo. Your horns are dented."

11

King Arclin II sat on his throne and meditated.

He meditated on the throne itself, which was nice enough in its way, but only temporary until his artisans were finished the big gold one with the etchings and bas-reliefs and fancy scrollwork and jewels.

He meditated on meeting the famous Hercules that afternoon, and hoped the big ox wasn't going to try anything stupid. He knew the man suspected all was not as it appeared in the kingdom. He also knew the man would probably have to die before the Grand Scheme had all its parts in place. It didn't bother him. People died. It was the way of life.

He meditated on the throne again, just long enough to order someone to bring him a cushion because this wood was getting pretty hard on his royal buttocks.

He meditated on the Grand Scheme. It wasn't terribly elaborate, and, in fact, hadn't been grand, or even a scheme, for that matter, until Zorin had let him know of a certain recent acquisition, which, unless the king was amenable to plans and schemes, would make sure the king wouldn't be king for much longer.

But the king, being the king, wasn't as stupid as some thought he was because of his height. Which, he insisted, wasn't so much short as it was compact and chock full with potential.

He went along with Zorin's plan because it suited him. And because it had done wonders for the treasury.

The plan, however, became a scheme, and a grand one at that, while Zorin was off on some filthy little battlefield, getting muddy and bloody and all the rest of the stuff that comes with being on a battlefield.

Arclin's battlefield, however, was the battlefield of the mind.

He had one; Zorin had one, too, but Zorin's mind was not as agile or twisted or clever as his.

Why, just this evening, as word of Drethic's acceptance of his sovereignty spread—with a little help from the king's runners—two more not inconsiderable communities had offered to enter into negotiation for voluntary assimilation. And one worried ruler had threatened him with dire consequences should he accept those offers.

Arclin wasn't worried.

The ruler had a pretty fair army.

Arclin, however, had Zorin and Zorin's Fire.

Which, when the Grand Scheme was nearly done, would then be known as Arclin's Fire.

He laughed.

Loudly.

His retinue laughed with him. Loudly.

Until the captain of the guard, quivering with fear, entered the throne room, dropped on his knees, and announced that the raider prisoners taken only this day had escaped from their inescapable confines.

"They . . . what?" Arclin boomed, which was something he had been practicing practically forever, since usually, when he got mad, he squeaked.

"Escaped, sire," the captain said, wincing in anticipated pain.

"Have you sent a patrol after them?"

"Yes, sire. But they've been gone quite a while."

Angrily Arclin rose from the throne, whose substantial dais allowed him to tower over the rest of the court. "Do you anticipate success, Captain?"

"My men will do their best," the man replied simply, and bravely.

Arclin glared.

The court glared.

The captain quailed.

Arclin thought the man was overdoing it a little, but no one else seemed to notice. He sighed resignedly to be sure the others understood that the weight of ruling lay heavily upon his shoulders, sank back onto his throne, and said, "Very well, Captain. All we can ask in these troubled times is that our brave men in uniform do their level best. As soon as you have word, come to me again."

The captain rose, bowed, and backed out of the room.

Arclin waited precisely twenty-six seconds before he looked around and said, "So. Is it just me, or is it chilly in here?"

Zorin paced his tent, hands clasped behind his back, gaze on the ground.

By this time, Theo and his men would have been freed from the king's jail. Given the distance, he didn't expect them back in camp until at least noon tomorrow. Yet he couldn't help wishing he knew now what they brought with them—the message he had been waiting for, or the message he dreaded.

Despite the late hour, he could hear others moving around outside. They were restless. They hadn't really been on the road since Drethic had been threatened and taken without so much as a single punch. Disappointment had lowered their morale. Fighting was what they did, and they did it well. They always took surrender badly.

"You're going to wear yourself out," Crisalt observed with a grin. He sat on the bottom step of Zorin's dais, legs crossed, hands loosely clasped against his stomach. "Have something to eat."

"I don't want anything to eat," Zorin snarled. "I want to know."

"We all want to know," Crisalt answered patiently. "But we can't know until they get here."

"I know, I know."

"So sit down. Or go beat someone up. You're driving me nuts."

Zorin whirled, a hand on the hilt of his sword, taking no satisfaction in the fleeting alarm that passed over his lieutenant's face. Unfortunately, he was right. But it didn't stop him from pacing. That was the only thing that kept him from going outside and beating someone up. That was even worse for morale than not fighting.

Crisalt cleared his throat. "There is good news, you know."

Zorin stopped.

"Hercules and his innkeeper friend are on their way back to Markan."

Zorin shook his head.

"What? You don't think that's good news? That Hercules is gone?"

"It only delays the inevitable, Crisalt."

"Yes, but why ask for more trouble? You'll get

him sooner or later. In this case, if I may say so, later is probably better."

Again Zorin knew his lieutenant was right, but it didn't make him feel any better. For his plan to work, for him to continue to work with that miserable little ant of a king until he chose the time to end the alliance, he required as little opposition as possible.

Hercules was not little opposition.

As long as he was out there, nothing would be certain.

Success would be tenuous at best.

"What I want to know," Crisalt drawled, "is why Hephaestos hasn't come for his toy."

Zorin's teeth gleamed through the depths of his beard.

That was easy. What the Armorer of the Gods had created was not just a toy, as Crisalt had put it. It was a weapon. And the weapons the gods used could be used not only against man, but against each other.

The gods may be immortal, but when the fire was loose, immortality didn't . . . well, it didn't last forever.

No; to protect himself he would have someone do his dirty work for him.

Zorin was convinced that that someone would be Hercules, which was the only reason why he had had a glorified shepherd like Theo attack the village where Hecules had been staying.

He took a deep breath, released it slowly, and sank wearily onto the nearest fur-covered stool. He drew his sword and watched the fire's reflection on the polished blade. "You know, Crisalt, sometimes I wish we were farmers. Nothing to worry about but getting the crops in on time, feeding the cattle, watering the horses, having kids, and fixing the house up now and then."

Crisalt agreed. "It's a lot simpler, that's for sure."

"And safer."

"Oh, yes, much safer."

Zorin stabbed the ground softly. "A wife."

"Oh, my, yes. A wife."

He held the sword up to his face and looked around it to his friend. "But we wouldn't get to kill anyone, would we?"

Crisalt shook his head.

"No blood."

"Nope."

"No entrails."

"Nope."

Zorin grinned. "No fun."

Crisalt grinned. "Absolutely no fun."

Zorin stood abruptly. "Okay, you win. Go fetch me someone to beat up. Promise him double rations and triple pay. This waiting is killing me."

• • •

Nikos dreamed of an inn filled with customers, all pushing gold into his hands, while Lydia skipped expertly between the tables, flirting with the men, laughing with the women, all the while having no eyes for anyone but him.

He dreamed of Bestor growing up to be Hercules.

He dreamed of having more children, and not really caring if they turned into urchins as long as they didn't have his honker of a nose.

He dreamed of birds flying overhead, their wings soft in the air, touching his cheeks, caressing his brow, flitting across his eyelids until they opened and he saw the underside of the leaves overhead, the firelight, and Hermes, looking down at him.

They were alone.

"Sleep well?" the messenger asked.

Nikos sat up and rubbed his eyes. "I guess so." He frowned. "But where's Hercules? And it's still night."

"Hercules is gone," Hermes told him. "And yes, it's still night."

"Gone?" Nikos scrambled to his feet. "Where gone? How gone? Why didn't he take me with him?"

Hermes passed the caduceus over the fire, which died instantly, leaving them in gentle moonlight.

"He has to save the world or something," he said, and chuckled. "You can help him by going home. Your Lydia is waiting, remember?"

114

"Home? Lydia?"

Hermes frowned. "Excuse me, but are we speaking the same language here?"

Nikos felt a touch of panic. "But I don't have any protection. I'll be attacked by raiders or bandits before I get halfway there. I'll be killed!"

"I know," Hermes said dryly. "You're not a fighter, you're an innkeeper."

"That's right." Nikos grabbed his cloak, took two steps toward the road, and stopped. He looked over his shoulder. "But you know, it would have been nice. Just once."

"Trust me," Hermes said. "It wouldn't have been. It never is." He shook himself, straightened his tunic, adjusted his belt, and held out one hand. "So, are you ready?"

"Ready? For what?"

Hermes rolled his eyes. "I hate to say this to a friend of Hercules, friend, but sometimes mortals can be truly dense." He waggled his hand until Nikos took it. "I'm taking you home, all right? I promised Hercules I'd see you there safely, and I will."

Nikos looked him over nervously. "That's wonderful. I guess. But—whoa!"

He looked down; he was flying. Or rather, he was holding desperately onto Hermes' hand while Hermes flew, all six wings beating the air furiously.

"Simple rules," Hermes explained, swinging them

115

gently westward. "You hold on, you won't fall. You fall, I'm not going to catch you because I already have a bad back and it's killing me."

Nikos held on.

He closed his eyes, however, because he didn't think he could stand looking into the dark down there while knowing that the dark down there was, in fact, down there. He also didn't think hitting it during a fall would be any fun.

Nor was he comforted when he heard Hermes mutter, "Demigod or no demigod, if Hercules gets out of this one alive, it'll be a bloody miracle."

12

"Now this is the way it works," Hercules said. "When we get there, you'll tell the guards you and the other men were separated in the dark, you got lost, and found me wandering around. You captured me—"

Theo the Mangler snorted his disbelief.

Hercules agreed, although not too quickly to be insulting. "Okay, you're probably right. So tell them I captured you and demanded that you take me to Zorin. That way you won't get into any more trouble than you already are. Maybe it'll even help."

"You don't know Zorin."

At Hercules' insistence they moved across the plain at a steady trot, although to Theo's mind it was more of an all-out run-like-hell-and-don't-trip. He wasn't used to this kind of sustained physical effort, and he had told Hercules that at least a dozen times. Not that Hercules would listen. Oh, no. All *he* wanted to do was get them *both* killed because of some ridiculous deadline or other which, if it passed, would cause all of them to die anyway.

So far, he hadn't been able to fathom what the deadline was.

On the other hand, the way things had worked out, he could already be dead anyway, so it didn't make much difference.

Getting out of the king's cell had been no problem. From what his friends had told him, it never was.

That smug captain of the guard was on constant lookout for prisoners like him. Which was to say, one of Zorin's soldiers. When the capture was made, a few dinars changed hands here and there along the chain of jail-guard command, and in the middle of the night a few days later, prisoners vanished mysteriously, only to turn up safe and sound at the valley camp. Or wherever the raiders happened to be at the time of the mysterious disappearance.

He often wondered what King Arclin's people thought. So many went in, and hardly anyone came out; surely they didn't believe the belowground cells held that many prisoners.

On the other hand, they had him for a king, so he supposed anything could happen.

Twice he tried to tell Hercules that they didn't have

to rush, the king's men wouldn't be after them, and twice the only answer was, "Don't slow down."

He didn't.

He didn't dare.

He didn't want that . . . that creature to come out of the night and pick him up again. That had been horrible. Terrifying. One moment he was hotfooting across the plain, admittedly lost and hoping he was heading in the right direction; the next moment he was flying, then falling, then sitting up to stare into the not very friendly eyes of the famous Hercules.

It was symbolic, so to speak, of his rotten luck.

As he had told Hercules, he wasn't really a raider. He was more of a guard, actually. Of cattle, to be honest. His job was to make sure the cattle didn't get away before they were eaten or turned into leather. It was, he had always believed, a special kind of skill. Not everyone could do it. Half the time the new boys ran themselves ragged chasing a stupid cow, only to have it turn out to be a not so stupid bull. He had lost more men that way. It was a trial.

But one morning the great Zorin himself had come to the herd's corral and had asked if he had ever wished he were a raider. A fighter. A man of action. Out there with the boys, hacking and slashing.

Theo had been so taken aback, he had actually blurted, "Yes, sir, I sure have."

Next thing he knew he was leading a small raiding

party on a town called Markan. The next thing he knew after that he was riding as a prisoner in a wagon to the jail. All because of Hercules.

It was enough to make him wonder if Zorin hadn't planned it all along.

"Keep up," Hercules urged, his voice not quite so harsh now.

"I'm trying," Theo gasped. "Really, I'm trying."

Truth be told, he was too frightened not to. He had seen what Hercules could do, had seen the look on the man's face when Theo had confessed that the Mangler part of the Theo the Mangler name was his own invention. But what choice had he had? It would hardly do for the bards to tell the tale of how Markan had been taken by Theo the Cattle Chaser, now would it.

Eventually, however, he could no longer put one foot in front of the other. He stumbled, fell, and when he discovered he could barely kneel, much less stand, Hercules scooped him up as if he were a child and carried him to the base of a gnarled, split-trunk tree whose lower branches were so heavy they nearly scraped the ground.

Hercules lowered him so that his back was against the trunk, and rubbed his own shoulder thoughtfully while he stared eastward. The moon was low in the sky, its light faint and gray, but Theo had no doubt what the man was looking at. Not particularly liking the dark, he managed to start a small fire with his flint and some twigs. There wasn't much warmth, but at least there was light.

"I don't think this is going to work," he said at last.

Hercules nodded without turning around.

"They're going to kill me, you know." Theo plucked a handful of grass and began to shred it, tossing the pieces angrily over his shoulder. "He was probably going to do it anyway. He never wanted me to be part of the fighting army." He grabbed another handful. "He used me." He looked up. "To get at you."

Hercules nodded. "Maybe."

Theo's temper shortened. "And you're going there anyway? You want me dead that much?"

Hercules pushed a hand back through his hair and sat in front of him. "I don't want you dead at all, Theo."

"Oh, sure. That's why you're taking me back there."

"All I need," Hercules said, "is a way in. After that, you're on your own."

Theo didn't believe it.

"It's true," Hercules assured him. "All I need is to get in." He looked around, grabbed a stick, and used the side of his hand to clear the earth between them. Then he handed Theo the stick. "Draw me a map of the camp. Everything you can think of. Show me Zorin's headquarters.''

It wasn't a request.

My luck, Theo thought miserably as he turned the stick over in his hand; my rotten luck.

Hercules watched the man sketch the camp's main points, pausing now and then to picture it in his mind. He said nothing beyond an occasional noise of encouragement, but he couldn't help thinking that should he make it through this, Hephaestos was going to owe him a truly huge debt.

And the more he thought about it, the angrier he grew.

It was as if, even without realizing it, everyone wanted to take advantage of him. Of his strength, and of his good nature.

And while he understood full well that he had chosen this life, and did not expect any reward for his deeds, it would be nice now and then if someone, anyone, would at least say "Please."

He almost laughed.

Theo glanced at him, puzzled.

Impatiently Hercules motioned him to continue, knowing it would be impossible to explain to the poor guy that he was not, after all, very good at feeling sorry for himself.

This wasn't the same as when he thought of his lost

wife and children. This was . . . well, perhaps not unreasonable but certainly pretty dumb.

"And this," Theo said, stabbing the earth at the top of his map, "is Zorin's tent. Black, with flags on it. Maybe a hundred and fifty paces from where the valley comes together in a V at the back. The walls are straight up," he added. "Not even a mountain goat could climb it."

Hercules studied the map for several minutes. It was crude, but there would only be one chance at this, and he needed all the information he could get.

He asked a few questions—the arrangement of living quarters, the mood of the men, the heaviest concentration of weapons, and what kind they were—which Theo, to his mild surprise, responded to without a second's hesitation. In fact, he offered so much information without prompting that Hercules couldn't help but be suspicious. True, the man by his own admission wasn't an army regular, and knew he had been used to draw Hercules into whatever Zorin and the king had in mind for this land, but he was still technically an enemy.

Hercules had no real way to know which part of this information was true, and which part was false enough to be deadly.

"Look," he said, "I need to—" and suddenly raised his head sharply.

Footsteps, and hushed voices.

Theo made to brush dirt over the fire, but Hercules stopped him. It was too late.

"Come on, swine," a harsh voice said loudly. "We know you're here. Show yourself, and we'll make it easy." A snigger. "Real easy."

Hercules spotted them—four men moving confidently along the faint trail he and Theo had used. Men in armor; men with weapons.

The king's men.

He glanced at Theo, who was still too exhausted to do much but try to push himself through the trunk to the other side. So much for the idea that the king never chased Zorin's so-called escaped raiders.

"Hey, a fire!"

Hercules eased back into the shadows.

The king's men stopped, the expression on their faces demonic, the metal on their armor seeming to glow a faint red. One of them ducked under a branch, and grinned.

"Well, well." His sword was drawn, and it was stained. "So you're going to make it easy."

A second soldier joined him.

Theo said, "Where are the others? My friends?"

The man's barking laugh was answer enough.

"Got lost, did you?" the second soldier said.

The first one whipped his sword back and forth lazily. "Get up, you swine. I don't like killing a man who won't at least stand on his own two feet."

"Good," Hercules said, sliding into the gap behind them. "Then we'll do it one at a time. Me first."

They spun around, but not fast enough.

Hercules grabbed the first by sword wrist and belt, lifted him over his head and whirled, and tossed him easily into the others waiting back on the trail. Before the second had managed to reach for his weapon, Hercules lashed out a stiff arm, catching him squarely across the chest. The man grunted and went down, and didn't move.

Three quick strides took Hercules to the tangled pile. He reached down, grabbed two heads, and slammed them together. The only sound this time was the faint crack of two skulls.

The remaining soldier scrambled backward before Hercules could reach him. He staggered to his feet, breathing heavily, sword in hand.

"You're not one of Zorin's," he said, wiping blood from his mouth.

Hercules smiled. "Thank you."

The man growled and began to shift right, then left, keeping Hercules between himself and the fire, the sword constantly moving.

Hercules feinted a charge and dropped back just before the tip punctured his chest; another feint, another retreat.

The sword, constantly moving.

"My friend is behind you," Hercules said mildly.

For an answer the soldier drew a long dagger as well, but he didn't turn around; he didn't take the bait.

He lunged, stopping instantly when Hercules dodged sharply left, sword tip and dagger following him. Another lunge, another stop.

They circled each other then, the only sounds the scuffling of their feet, the hiss of the sword as it lashed the air, the harsh rasp of the soldier's breath as he sought an opening, the creak of his leather.

Hercules kept his attention on the man's eyes, using his peripheral vision to keep track of the blades. What he saw wasn't encouraging. The man knew exactly what he was doing, and knew he could keep this game up until his opponent lost patience, or grew tired, or grew too bold. He wouldn't be the one who would make the first move.

Hercules feinted; the soldier didn't even flinch.

Circling; always circling.

It wasn't long before Hercules felt a faint but unmistakable weariness in his limbs, a slowly increasing weight that threatened to blunt his reactions. Not because of this dance, but because he had had barely no sleep the night before, had suffered the long journey today, the run . . . it was all catching up, and catching up fast.

The man appeared to sense it.

He smiled.

The sword dared him; the dagger taunted him.

And something large rose out of the dark behind him.

The soldier sensed the danger and started to turn, the sword whipping around ahead of him, stabbing into the darkness. There was a quiet grunt before a length of dead branch split in half across the soldier's skull and he went down where he stood, the sword spinning away into the dark, the dagger still in his hand.

Theo dropped the makeshift club as Hercules walked over.

"Is he dead?" the raider asked.

Hercules knelt beside the fallen man. "I don't know. Close enough, I would think."

"Good." Theo's voice sounded older, harder. "Now, if you don't mind, I'd like to get some rest."

"Not here," Hercules said.

"Wherever," Theo answered, and walked away.

Hercules waited patiently until he heard the man collapse again. He grinned, found him, and was about to pick him up when he heard a faint moan. Frowning, he knelt, inhaling sharply when he saw the sheen of sweat on the man's face, and the blood that seeped from his side into the earth.

"Not fast enough," Theo said, grimacing. When Hercules leaned closer, hands out to strip off his bloodstained clothes, Theo held a wrist. "No sense, Hercules. I've seen damage like this before." His eyes

127

closed tightly, his lips pulled away from his teeth.

Helpless and angry, Hercules prepared himself to wait.

It didn't take that long.

Theo paled. His breathing caught, eased, caught again. "Basher," he whispered, trying to smile.

Hercules gripped his arm. "Yes."

"Much better than Cattle Chaser or Mangler."

"It suits you, friend."

Theo turned his head, young face old as pain made the flesh and muscles taut. "Really?"

Hercules nodded.

"Then . . . we're even. For what I did, I mean."

"Not quite," Hercules told him. "You saved my life."

Theo didn't answer.

He couldn't.

Hercules bowed his head for a moment, rubbed a weary hand across his face, and sighed. A look into the dark, then:

"A favor, Hades," he whispered to the night as he folded Theo's hands on his chest. "Treat him well. He was no warrior. Except when he had to be. Treat him well, he deserves it."

Beyond the firelight, deep in the shadows, a shimmering dark much blacker than the night around it.

And a deep voice that answered gently: "I'll see to it, my friend. Don't worry."

13

Hercules knew himself to be a reasonably even-tempered man. He had his flashes of temper, of course, just like anyone else, but for the most part violent eruptions were not part of his nature. He did not like the lack of control they signified.

On those rare occasions when he became enraged, however, there was less an explosion than there was a deep-seated coldfire that deepened his voice and narrowed his eyes and made him more aware than ever of what his great strength could do.

He slept that night without dreams.

When he awoke, the coldfire was there. As much a part of him now as the flesh on his bones.

He walked toward the twin mountains along a narrow gritty trail that wound across the plain's increasingly uneven ground. Brush and thorned bushes took over much of the grass; small groves of wind-bent trees huddled like tiny islands along dried creek beds; the few birds he spotted flew in all directions but west.

He had no clear idea of exactly what he would do once he reached Zorin's hidden valley, but whatever it was, he vowed Zorin wouldn't like it very much. He also realized that he was probably being more than a little foolish. One man against an army, and a ruthless army at that. Maybe he ought to have a plan first. Do this, do that, have this backup and that fallback.

The trouble with his plans were, however, that few of them ever worked the way they were supposed to. People seldom did what his plans wanted them to, and he usually ended up improvising anyway, so why bother with a plan in the first place?

He grinned.

He squinted against the bright sun and watched the plain begin to rise toward the mountains.

It wasn't difficult to locate the place where the valley's entrance ought to be. And from the thick clouds that hovered over the one on the left, he suspected that that was where Hephaestos' summer forge was located.

Which gave him an idea.

Suppose he just went to Hephaestos first? The armorer wasn't as inflexible as his reputation sometimes suggested. He could be talked to. He was always open to reasonable persuasion, the exchange of ideas, the notion of compromise, the give-and-take of negotiation. A few words, a pleasant meal, a full stomach, and surely Hephaestos would give up this stupid idea of creating another volcano just because some idiot had stolen something of his.

Hercules smiled, and his step became a bit lighter.

And if he wouldn't give up the volcano-destruction idea, well, then, deadlines can be extended, terms agreed to, specifics hammered out, and in the meantime no one dies.

He almost laughed aloud as he entered a long, thin band of sycamores.

And as a last resort, he could always get Aphrodite on his side. Hephaestos never refused his wife anything, and she would certainly understand that Hercules was arguing from a strong position, a position of logic, a position of power.

He had seen her influence before.

It was formidable.

It was scary, too.

Maybe bringing her into it wouldn't be such a great idea. Especially if she sided with her husband.

All right, all right, he decided, we'll go with the first plan. I'll talk with Hephaestos, make him see that there are other ways to get what you want besides blowing up half a kingdom, and together we'll bring Zorin to his knees. No problem.

"Halt!"

On the other hand . . .

Four heavily armed men stepped onto the path in front of him. Behind him four more stepped out of the trees; these held spears whose tips appeared obscenely sharp, and aimed at such portions of his anatomy as to make him revise his instant plan to take them all on.

"What are you doing here?" one of the men in front demanded.

Improvise, he ordered himself; use those instincts your mother claims are so godlike.

"I want to see Zorin," he said calmly.

The men laughed.

"And what makes you think he'll see you?"

"Because my name is Hercules, and I understand he's looking for me."

The laughter stopped.

Hercules folded his arms across his chest and waited. He had no idea why his instincts had directed him to say that, but he was willing to trust them for a while longer. At least long enough, he realized too late, for one of the spears to be placed lightly against the back of his neck, another in the small of his back, and a third under the point of his chin.

With no incentive to struggle, he allowed his arms to be bound behind his back and his ankles to be tethered, so that his stride was shortened to half its usual length. Once he was secured, the raiders marched him out of the trees and toward a high gate set between the mountains.

None of them spoke.

He didn't even try. He supposed he could have eventually burst the tether and shredded the bonds, and maybe even bested these men if they were willing to come at him only one or two at a time. The problem was those spears, whose tips continued to press against various parts of his back. One twitch, and he was punctured.

Not to mention those archers on the top of the gate.

Plans and improvisations, he thought sourly; but at least I'm going to see Zorin. One step closer to getting what I want.

An hour later, still bound, still guarded, he told himself to shut up.

The tent was small, with no center pole, just one at each corner. The ground was hard and worn bare. Bundles of furs and hides were stacked unevenly around the walls, and Hercules had been dumped against one such pile at the back. He lay on his side, head aching from a thump with the butt of a spear, given for no other reason than the fact that he was who he was.

He didn't move.

There was no need; not now.

He had been brought directly here by the guards, and was pleased to see that Theo's map had been, for the most part, accurate. The camp was laid out in ranks and files on both sides of the shallow stream, wide "streets" between them; meals were apparently taken in a communal area near the pond; the livestock were kept at the base of the south slope. As best he could tell, the valley was close to half a mile wide, twice that deep. Easily large enough to accommodate what Zorin needed.

Theo had said the back slope was nearly vertical, and smooth; what he hadn't said was that the others were virtually the same. Bare gray rock glinting now and then with chips of mica; a rare spot of green where a scrawny bush tried to take hold; their height at least one hundred feet before they angled away to their respective peaks.

A slight tremor took the valley floor as he was pushed toward his temporary jail, but no one took any visible notice. Not even the horses seemed upset.

When he asked about Zorin, no one responded.

Midday came and went. No attempt had been made to feed him or give him water.

Outside he could hear two guards complaining, gossiping, joking with those who passed and wanted to know if it was really Hercules inside and was he as fearsome as legend told it.

Evidently not, from the scornful laughter he also heard.

Eavesdropping also told him the camp was seldom at full strength. Smaller bands of raiders were constantly on the move, their size dependent on their current target. Activity had been more frequent over the past two months, and there were many objections to the lack of rest time between missions. Even now parties were out, leaving the area more than half empty.

Finally he shifted, tensing against the anticipated pain in his head. When it failed to happen, he wriggled into a sitting position, his back against a bundle of furs, his legs outstretched.

By this time he had become attuned to the noise and rhythm of the camp. Aside from the guards, he could hear men marching, the distant lowing of cattle, the telltale creak of carts and wagons, the clash of swords and other weapons in practice sessions.

By midafternoon he had taken to calling to the guards every ten or fifteen minutes, demanding something to eat, something to drink. They ignored him as long as they could, then popped in one at a time to threaten him with scowls and staffs, swords and daggers; he noticed, however, that not one of them came within reach of his legs.

Small satisfaction, but he took it, because he knew Zorin was trying to wear him down. Letting him wait.

Letting him suffer. Hoping he'd be more amenable when their meeting finally occurred.

It was no surprise, then, when he at last had a visitor, long after daylight had been replaced by the uneven glow of torches and pit fires.

The visitor was a man of medium height, with a broad chest, brawny arms and legs, his hair and beard a deep disturbing red. He wore boots laced up to his knees, heavy leather pants, and an open leather vest.

He carried no weapon that Hercules could see.

He did, however, bring a small jug of water and a plate of bread and meat chunks. These he set at Hercules' feet before sitting cross-legged on the ground, his back to the entrance.

"I think you must be hungry," he said in a voice edged with gravel.

"You must think I'm a magician," Hercules answered with a smile, "if you expect me to eat that like this." He rocked to underscore the bindings of his arms.

"Crisalt," the man said by way of introduction. "And you must be Hercules."

"I'm still not a magician."

Without turning around, Crisalt barked an order, and an extremely nervous guard scuttled in, hesitated, then reached behind Hercules and cut the rope. Hercules thanked him, unsettling the guard even more, and rubbed the life back into his wrists and forearms.

As he did so, he saw the sword the guard placed in Crisalt's lap as he left.

Still smiling, he leaned forward quickly to take the jug and plate, holding back a laugh when Crisalt's hand instantly covered the hilt.

The water was warm, the meat tough; he had no complaints.

Unless, he thought suddenly, it's poisoned.

"You don't have anything to worry about," Crisalt told him with mild amusement. "Zorin is much more direct."

Hercules ate, drank, examined the man who sat before him. Unlike poor Theo, this one was a true warrior. Although the light in the tent had begun to dim, he could see along the man's arms, and on his face and neck the tiny pocks and scars of more than a few battles. Although he was heavy, he was probably also quite quick.

"So when do I get to see Zorin?"

"In good time. He wants to know why you're here."

Hercules shrugged, wiping the back of a hand across his mouth. "I heard he wanted to see me."

Crisalt frowned his suspicion. "Just like that?"

"Why not?" He finished the meat, and mopped up the last of the gravy with the last of the bread. "I understand he's a pretty good leader."

"Oh. And I suppose you want to join him?"

"Oh, no," Hercules said. "Oh, no."

It was Hercules' turn to be amused as he watched Crisalt try to unravel the puzzle, running through all the possibilities, the dangers, the threats, and coming up empty. He was a direct man, like most soldiers, and when something didn't make any sense, it was considered treacherous ground.

Hercules wouldn't give him the satisfaction of letting him know he was right.

Another tremor, this one not strong enough to raise dust or stir a feather.

It was in the bones, and Hercules knew Hephaestos was growing increasingly impatient.

There were three days left in the ultimatum; he doubted the armorer would wait even that long.

Crisalt snapped another order over his shoulder, and this time five men entered the tent, each gawking at Hercules, each doing his best to hide behind the other without actually moving.

"You're finished," Crisalt pointed out.

Hercules agreed that he was, and accommodated the guards by putting his arms behind his back and half turning so they could retie him without having to get too close. It took them so long Crisalt had to threaten several disgustingly effective punishments if they didn't hurry up.

They did, and left so fast Hercules felt the breeze.

"Most men are cowards," Crisalt said with a sneer

at the guards' backs. "They need strong men to lead them into courage."

"Like Zorin?"

"Exactly."

"And maybe King Arclin?"

"The man is a pest, nothing more."

Lie, Hercules thought.

"If it wasn't for those men of his, we'd have the whole country by now."

Lie, Hercules thought.

Crisalt reached into his vest and pulled out a small dagger, its hilt carved from bone. He used it to pick at a scab on his wrist. "So tell me again, Hercules—why are you here?"

"To see Zorin."

"But not to join him."

"No."

Crisalt smiled at the drop of blood he had pricked from his skin. "To kill him?"

"With an entire army around? I'm not that stupid."

Oh, really? a silent voice asked; *so how come you're tied up again? How come you walked in here without even a plan? Give me a minute, I'll think of another word for* stupid.

"I don't understand," Crisalt said, lifting his wrist to lick off the blood.

"You don't have to," Hercules answered politely. "Only Zorin does. No offense."

"Oh, none taken, Hercules, none taken." He put the dagger away, dropped his hand over the sword. "But until you tell me why you want to see Zorin, I'm afraid you'll have to stay here."

"A waiting game? Who breaks first?"

Crisalt stared. "Zorin doesn't play games. You'd better understand that. He doesn't play games."

Hercules leaned back against the furs and drew his knees up. "Whatever you say."

Oh good, the silent voice said as Crisalt rose and tapped the sword against his palm; *taunt the man, why not, make him lose his temper. You call this a plan?*

Hercules kept his expression neutral, not looking at the sword, only at the man's face.

Finally Crisalt snarled wordlessly and stomped out, loudly ordering the guards to cut Hercules' throat if he so much as moved a single muscle.

Hercules waited.

Crisalt returned, his face nearly as red as his beard. "I'll tell you something, Hercules. Zorin won't play games with the likes of you."

"You already said that," Hercules reminded him mildly.

Crisalt took a step forward, glared, and stomped out again, this time ordering the guards to cut him into little pieces if he even so much as blinked a single eye.

Hercules waited.

Crisalt returned, sword drawn and trembling with his anger. "I'll give you a hint. You'll wish Zorin had killed you straight off before he's done with you."

Hercules remembered the feel of Theo's blood on his hand, the sight of Markan's dead in the square.

Still he said nothing. He had pushed this man as far as he dared, and pushed no more.

When Crisalt left the third time, no orders were given, although he did hear one guard yelp.

A minute later he inhaled slowly and released the tension with his breath. And he whispered, "I don't think so, friend. I really don't think so."

14

The captain of the guard stood outside the throne room and dusted various parts of his armor, took off his helmet and tucked it under his arm, fussed with his hair, and closed his eyes in brief prayer. He hoped he looked all right. It wouldn't do for a man of his position to spend the last moments of his life looking like something dragged behind a jackass through a pigsty. And make no mistake about it, these were indeed the last moments of his life. When King Arclin heard what he had to report, there was no question he would be sent straight to the underworld on the fastest available chariot. He wouldn't even have to bother packing.

The door opened slowly.

He drew himself up, muttered another prayer, and marched into the room, his footsteps echoing faintly.

Aside from his king, he was the only one there.

And only a single torch burned, just to the left of the throne.

"Well?" the king demanded.

The captain told him.

Arclin fumed. "All of them?"

The captain of the guard shook his head. "No, sire. One survives intact. Another survives, but it appears as if he will never be the same."

The king scowled, leaned back on the throne, and passed a thoughtful hand over his chin. "You have no doubt who did this to your men?"

"None, sire." The captain began to hope; just a little. "We found the body of one of the, uh, escaped prisoners nearby. He must have gotten separated from his mates during their flight from the city."

"But he wasn't alone?"

"I doubt it, sire. These were four good men, among the best we had. Handpicked, specially trained. There's only one place their attackers could have come from."

"And the other prisoners?"

The captain wanted to smile, but good sense overrode the impulse. "As you ordered, sire, as you ordered."

The king tented his fingers beneath his chin and stared at the floor.

The captain tried not to feel the definite chill that had entered the room.

"Well," the king said at last. He lifted his gaze. "It seems you have done all you can, Captain, under the circumstances."

The captain didn't even dare blink.

"You have failed me, of course."

"Yes, sire."

"Good men are dead because you failed."

"Yes, sire."

The king lowered his hands into his lap and clasped them loosely. "But you are, for the moment, too valuable to lose." A finger pointed. "Before you grow too confident, however, know that you only have one chance to redeem yourself, Captain. One chance, no more than that. So." He sniffed, studied the vaulted ceiling for a moment, and shook his head. "You will get a good night's sleep, rest your body and mind, and first thing in the morning you will meet with your lieutenants. You will talk, you will devise, and by nightfall, you will bring me a foolproof plan to take care of our . . . problem."

The captain swallowed. "Sire, if . . . if I may?"

The king nodded, very slowly.

"Sire, as much as I wish I could tell you differently, we're really not ready yet. Not for what you're suggesting. The men are still training. The armorers are still working. I don't even want to talk about that idiot making the chariots. Not to mention the—"

"Your spies," the king said as if the captain hadn't spoken, "tell you that the camp is only at half strength, yes? A little less, perhaps?"

I knew it, the captain thought dismally; I knew it.

"Yes, sire."

"Are you telling me, then, that half that swine's army is better than your men?"

"Of course not, sire!"

The king smiled. It was a terrible smile, even on a man as short as he. "Then by nightfall, Captain. You will come back to me by nightfall."

There was no room for protest. The captain bowed stiffly, made a smart about-face, and marched from the room. As soon as the door closed behind him, he sagged against the wall and wiped a torrent of sweat from his brow. He was alive, so he supposed he ought to be grateful. But he might as well be dead. Oh, there'd be a plan by nightfall, he wouldn't fail his king there. The problem was, that plan was going to get them all skewered, if not worse, by the point of Zorin's Fire.

Sleep, he thought glumly as he made his way toward his quarters; sure, right, and tomorrow I'm going to be the richest man in the kingdom.

Arclin remained in the throne room for over an hour, staring blindly at the dark walls. He had dismissed his

145

court because he didn't want them to see how apprehensive he was. He had to be strong. He had to be stern. He had to prove that he had the makings of a true king so they'd stop whispering about how things had changed since his father had died.

Again, he smiled that terrible smile.

Well, things were going to change, all right.

It didn't matter that the Grand Scheme had had to be pushed up a month or so. Once it was in place, by tomorrow night if that weasel captain wanted to draw another breath, nothing would stop it.

And nothing would stop him.

Nothing.

Crisalt dreaded going into the tent.

It had been bad enough sitting alone with Hercules, feeling the unnatural power that fairly rippled off the man's body, listening to his barely concealed sarcasm, watching him ignore every threat and intimidation. It galled. And he didn't even look like much—a little taller than average, maybe, and a bit more bulk here and there—but that *power* was enough to make a strong man quail.

Now he knew what Zorin had meant.

Bad enough, indeed.

Now, however, he had to go in there and tell his leader what he had just learned from a man who had lived only long enough to bring the news to the camp.

His wounds had been horrid, and Crisalt suspected they had been inflicted that way exactly so he'd be able to deliver the message and nothing more.

The outside guards looked at him oddly.

He snarled at them, tugged at his beard, and marched in.

Zorin was alone, and the fire in its pit was nearly out.

"Well?" Zorin demanded.

"I have news."

"Hercules?"

"Other news."

"Tell me."

He did, and braced himself.

As expected, Zorin lunged to his feet and bellowed, "That spineless little grub did *what*?"

"All but one, sir."

"Hunted down? Slaughtered? They had no weapons to protect them?"

"Yes. Defenseless."

Zorin's face reddened, and Crisalt was afraid the man would explode. Instead he dropped back into his chair and yanked angrily at his clothes, at his hair.

"Which one escaped?"

"Theo."

Zorin looked incredulous. "Theo? The Mangler?"

Crisalt nodded.

Zorin laughed and looked at the ceiling. "I don't suppose his body will be found?"

"I doubt it, sir. My guess is, he was able to get away during the fight."

Zorin nodded, cocked his head, and grinned. "I would bet he's halfway to Athens by now." He slapped a knee. "Well, good luck to him. Any man who escapes two death sentences in one day deserves another chance." A slow turn of his head, a sideways look. "Now tell me about Hercules."

Crisalt moved closer to his leader, pulled up a stool, and presumed to sit without invitation. "But what about Arclin?"

"Oh, I'm so afraid, Crisalt, can't you see I'm so afraid?" Zorin stared at the dying fire, and spat dryly at it. "When all the parties are back, old friend, we'll send him a little Fire. Meanwhile, I want to know about Hercules. What did he say, what did he do, why is he here?"

Crisalt told him, as simply and unemotionally as possible. Throughout the narration, Zorin nodded, or grunted, or stared at the ceiling, or plucked invisible things from the fur that lined his chair.

A bad sign.

Crisalt kept talking, but eased the stool back without, he hoped, seeming to do so.

When he was finished, Zorin looked at him for a

long time before saying, "If you had taken five more minutes, you'd be outside, you know."

Crisalt looked around sheepishly, grinned stupidly, and dragged the stool back to the center of the floor. "So what are you going to do with him?"

"Kill him."

"Just like that?"

"Just like that. My friend, Hercules is not a man to fool around with. You know that now, I can tell. Torture is fine for ordinary men. He is no ordinary man. So what you'll do is, as soon as you leave, surround the tent with your best men, as armed as they can get without falling over. Then take at least a score more, arm them, fetch Hercules, and bring him to me." He rubbed his palms together. "Then . . . we'll kill him."

Crisalt was disappointed. He understood the precautions because he had felt the power, but he had really hoped for a few minutes' recreation before the deed was done.

"I know, I know," Zorin said with a regretful nod and look. "But this is no time to take chances, Crisalt. The sooner Hercules is taken care of, the sooner we can pay a visit to our friend with the crown." An eyebrow lifted. "And then, I promise you, we'll have all the fun we can handle."

Crisalt rose at Zorin's gesture, gave him a friendly mocking bow, and hurried outside. Took a deep breath. Looked up at the stars and hoped one of them would be lucky enough to keep him alive long enough for him to have that promised fun.

He had a feeling that was one wish it would take a miracle to fulfill.

Restraining the urge to laugh, Zorin watched Crisalt leave, so stiff-legged it was clear the man wanted to run, not walk. But he didn't blame him. Things had come to a head much sooner, perhaps too much sooner, than either of them had anticipated. He had to give Arclin some credit, though—he didn't expect the tiny toad to have this much courage. Taunting Zorin by breaking their prisoner agreement. Daring him to do something about it when he obviously knew the raider camp was at less than half of full strength. Had Arclin been a foe worthy of even a modicum of respect, Zorin would have applauded him before personally stomping him into the ground.

As it was, he only promised himself to keep the king alive. Buried up to his neck, to be sure, in the middle of the courtyard of what would soon be Zorin's palace.

But alive.

While Zorin watched him starve to death. If, of course, the creatures under the earth didn't get to him first.

He grunted a laugh.

He rose, stretched, and wondered if he should have the Fire ready when Hercules was brought to him.

He grunted again.

Probably.

It always made him feel good when he saw the expression on a man's face, the expression that told him the man knew he was going to die.

On Hercules, the expression would be priceless.

15

There were times when Hercules wished he had some magic in him. Not a whole lot; just enough to make certain situations a little easier to bear. A wave of a wand like Hermes' caduceus, for example, and his enemies would be vanquished, his wounds healed, his life in general made a whole lot simpler.

He suspected, though, that a life like that, for a man like him, would also be unbearably dull.

Considering his current circumstances, however, maybe dull wouldn't be all that bad once in a while.

For the fifth time since Crisalt had left, he tested the strength of the rope that bound his wrists, straining to break it, snap it, even stretch it a little. It didn't work. His position was too awkward. Watching the entrance carefully, then, he pushed back against the furs behind him and tried to bring his hands down, under his rump, and out to the front.

He got as far as his rump before he overheard one guard question the other about maybe checking on their prisoner before Crisalt returned. The second guard, in as few words as possible, wanted to know if his friend had lost his tiny, and evidently nonfunctioning, mind. The prisoner was fine. The prisoner wasn't going anywhere. The guard had no intention of tempting fate, the gods, or Zorin by going in there and inadvertently doing something stupid.

The first guard grumbled a little and agreed.

Hercules agreed as well, braced his feet on the ground, and lifted himself just enough to ease his weight from his hands. His cheeks puffed as he blew a breath of relief before drawing his feet in close so he could slip his hands under them and up over his knees.

After that, it was easy.

His posturing earlier had made the guards too nervous when they had returned to retie him. The rope wasn't nearly as tight as it had been, and now it was just a matter of getting it off without alerting those outside that something was wrong.

He tried a simple snap; it didn't work.

He tried pulling his hands apart quickly, and all that

did was break a sweat across his brow and rub the rope harshly against his skin.

All right, so maybe a little magic wouldn't hurt.

Crisalt suggested to the guards in front of Zorin's headquarters that they leave their posts on peril of their lives, both here and in the underworld. Then he stomped off toward the main camp, muttering to himself, shaking his head, muttering some more, and finally stopping at a clutch of tents that housed the army's elite.

He picked six men, told them to arm themselves as if they were going to single-handedly attack Sparta and leave no survivors, and follow him.

They had two minutes to get ready, or he would make sure their families were told how brave they had been when they died.

Two minutes later he was on his way to get Hercules.

Again Hercules stared at the entrance, but this time he didn't see it. He didn't see anything. All his concentration centered on the rope, on the wrists, on the arms.

On the *power*.

The camp faded as if a pale cloud had settled over it; sound muted, movement paused, nothing left but silence.

A slow inhalation filled his chest as he imagined his arms drifting slowly apart. Biceps swelled, his face darkened, his forearms became rigid, and the rope began to strain. He could feel the individual strands stretch and tighten, could feel the burning they caused, could feel them separate from each other and stretch still more.

Crisalt and his men crossed the shallow stream.

He warned them that Hercules didn't look like much, but could take them all on without breathing heavily.

To a man they doubted it, and doubted it loudly.

Crisalt shrugged.

What he didn't tell them was the way he had felt when confronting Hercules.

What he didn't tell them was what he knew he would only admit to himself in nightmares.

What he didn't tell them was the fear.

And for making him feel that, Hercules would have to die. One way or another.

Hercules began to shake, just a little.

Sweat rolled down his arms, his spine.

The rope thinned.

The strands began to snap, one by one.

• • •

An empty, ox-drawn wagon lumbered across the path Crisalt intended to take. He swore at the driver, swore at the oxen, swore at the wagon, and suddenly had a bad feeling about the night.

Hercules sensed the bones in his wrists approach the breaking point, and with a near-silent grunt jerked, and pulled, and the rope finally fell away.

He sagged against the furs with a long sigh, blinked a few times to clear his vision, and hastily attacked the loose tether around his ankles. The knot had been sloppily tied, and it came undone without much effort, despite the clumsiness of his fingers. He flexed them to bring back their strength, stood, and almost immediately decided against leaving by the front door. There were too many men out there, and as swift as he could be, one of them would be bound to spot him.

Unfortunately his captors hadn't been thoughtful enough to leave him any weapons, and that magic he didn't have couldn't change his appearance.

What he needed was a little luck.

Hurry!'' Crisalt told his men.

They asked no questions.

They began to run.

Hercules seldom kidded himself when it came to fate. As much as he was pleased when good fortune tagged along on one of his journeys, he also knew that it could leave him without warning. This also made him realize that luck was largely a matter of determination; it was there if he just looked hard enough.

Such as the tent he was in, and how it would help him get out of here before they came to get him.

He grinned, and easily snapped a rawhide tie from around the bundle of fur he had been using as a brace. Seconds later he found one just barely long enough for use as a makeshift cloak. He tucked it under one arm, moved the stack aside, and tested the bottom of the tent.

It lifted easily.

"There!" Crisalt called, and pointed. "There it is!"

Wasting no more time, Hercules drew the pile back into place as best he could while at the same time he crawled out. It wouldn't fool anyone for very long, but even a second's advantage might be just what he needed.

He caped the newly treated fur around his shoulders and held it closed across his throat with his left hand. His dress would instantly peg him as an outsider, but here the setup of the camp itself worked in his favor. With the tents arranged in rows, and spaced several paces apart in makeshift streets, the single torches that burned before each did little to dispel the darkness.

He would be seen, yet only briefly, nothing more than a shadow that once in a while gained human form.

If he crouched to disguise his height, it would take a sharp-eyed raider indeed to realize this man wasn't one of theirs. Especially since he did not try to conceal himself, but walked as if with purpose, intent on following a commander's orders so he could get himself back to his bed.

Crisalt couldn't believe his rotten luck.

Neither would he admit to the others that he had counted wrong, and had brought them to the wrong place.

"Okay," he said curtly, as if he knew what he was talking about. "You've got the drill. Good. Now let's get him before Zorin slices us all."

As he led his men away, he knew this was going to cost him dearly just to keep their mouths shut. And just when he had enough to make the down payment on that retirement villa down south.

Hercules passed a small fire around which a half-dozen raiders gambled with ivory sticks and clay cups. They grumbled a greeting, he grunted one in return.

Farther on, to his right, he saw two men lounging by a fence, drinking from a bulging wineskin. On the other side of the fence he could see the shadowy figures of horses, the occasional glint of an eye, and heard one horse impatiently pawing the ground. Next to this corral was another that, by the sound and smell of it, held the oxen and cattle. One of the men called to him drunkenly, and he waved over his shoulder as he swung sharply left, soon finding himself at the stream Theo had told him parted the valley down its middle.

Isolated reflections of fire rippled across its surface; stars, he thought, that didn't quite make it to the heavens.

Another fifty yards brought him to the last of the soldiers' tents. The stream curved away into the dark to the left.

And directly ahead he saw Zorin's headquarters.

Crisalt's eyes bulged, his mouth opened to yell, and his right hand clutched his sword so tightly his fingers threatened to cramp.

The tent was down, the bundles of fur and hides unbound and scattered.

"Gone?" he gasped in disbelief.

The guards cowered.

"Gone?"

The guards glanced uneasily at each other, daring each other to remind the commander that he himself had ordered them not, under any circumstances, to go into the tent without him.

"Gone?"

The six elite shrugged; this, thank the gods, wasn't their problem.

Crisalt rounded on the guards, intending to behead them even as he remembered that he had ordered them to remain outside no matter what Hercules said, no matter what they might hear inside. But it would be a wasted effort. In truth, they weren't to blame, they were good men, and he would need all the good men he could find when Zorin found out.

One of the guards dared break the silence: "Shall we alert the gate, sir?"

He almost agreed, then changed his mind with an audible gulp. "By the gods," he whispered. "By the gods."

He knew were Hercules was headed.

The raider headquarters wasn't hard to miss, even though it was black.

A large open space separated it from the bulk of the camp. High torch poles placed ten yards apart fronted it, illuminating its size and underscoring its importance. The center flap was held up by two stout poles, like a canopy; flanking the entrance were four guards in full armor and full weaponry. They had no doubt been chosen for the dubious honor not only because of their skills, but because of their size.

Hercules decided walking right in probably wouldn't work.

Never easy, he grumbled to himself as he veered to his right, keeping as far away from the reach of the torches as he could; it's never easy, is it? It has to be hard. Like there's some kind of law that says I can't have it easy once in a while.

Yet finding a way to sneak into Zorin's tent would take time; and time was the one thing he had precious little of at the moment.

So if there was a law, it was about time he broke it.

Keeping his head down and the fur close around him, he passed between two torch poles and headed directly for the canopy. None of the guards spotted him until he was but a few paces away, and when they did, it was as if they had all seen him at the same time—they swiveled as one, swords drawn, shields up.

"Go away," was the simple command one of them gave.

Hercules mumbled, and kept walking.

"Hey, toad, you heard me—go away!"

Hercules hesitated, shuffling as if in confusion.

"Five seconds and you're dog meat."

Hercules didn't give them that long.

He tossed aside the cloak and grabbed the nearest guard's shield, yanking it free and clobbering him with it. Without pausing, he spun and slammed it into the face of the man next to him. The heel of a boot caught the third in the stomach, sending him instantly to his knees. The fourth guard managed one step before Hercules drew back his arm, whipped it forward, and let the shield do all the work.

The guard dropped.

One man remained—the guard still gasping for breath on his knees. "Sorry," Hercules said, and thumped him. The man grunted, swayed, and sagged the rest of the way to the ground.

Not pretty, but effective.

He ducked under the canopy and strode inside.

Zorin was in his chair. He looked up, glared, and said, "Who are you?"

Hercules glanced around, but didn't stop walking. "I was going to say I'm your worst nightmare, but after seeing this place, I've changed my mind."

Zorin's eyes widened. "Hercules!"

Closer: "I want the Fire."

Zorin gaped.

Closer: "I want it now."

Suddenly Zorin exploded into laughter, leaped from his chair, and vanished around the back.

In spite of himself, Hercules stopped.

"You want the Fire?" Zorin yelled. "You want the Fire?"

And the tent began to glow with a pulsing red light.

16

The Fire, in its simplicity, was nothing less than elegant.

Its blade was half as wide as other swords of its kind, and so highly polished it seemed to take on the color of whatever it was near. Its hilt was solid black, the grip designed as lightning bolts entwined about each other, while the cross guard was formed as a two-headed serpent.

But the design and reflection did not disguise the fact that it also had two deadly edges, not just one.

There were no jewels, no gaudy ornamentation, which only served to highlight how exquisite it was, and how deadly.

The fire-red glow came not from the metal itself, nor from the blade, but from some distant fire drawn to it whenever it was exposed.

Zorin stood before his chair and held the Fire in front of him, tip aimed at the ceiling. His face gleamed; his eyes were nearly shut. On the seat behind him was a limp leather sheath that shone blackly, as though it had been saturated with expensive oils.

"You want it?" he asked softly. "You come get it."

He lowered the tip as he took a step down, and brushed it across the ground.

A trail of low fire burned along the trail.

Zorin's smile dared Hercules to make his move.

"Hephaestos wants it back," Hercules said.

Zorin shook his head as he stepped to the ground. "He can't have it. It's mine."

"You're making a mistake, Zorin."

"Oh no, Hercules, it's you who's made the mistake." The sword slowly, very slowly, parted the air between them. "This is my country here. In this valley. You are the invader. And invaders must die."

A subterranean rumble raised puffs of dust around the edges of the pit, the edges of the tent.

Raised voices outside were alarmed, while others sounded angry and urgent.

Hercules shook his head. "I'm telling you, Zorin, Hephaestos won't stand for it much longer."

"Then he'll have to come and get it, won't he?"

Hercules couldn't believe the man's arrogance. Surely he understood what the tremors presaged;

surely he couldn't ignore what Hephaestos could do if he were provoked.

Zorin eyed the Fire lovingly, his free hand caressing the length of the blade without actually touching it. "This is a god's sword. And it's a god killer."

Hercules held out his right hand. "The Fire, Zorin."

Zorin started to laugh, caught himself, and instead stretched his arm out, bringing the Fire's tip within inches of Hercules' palm.

The heat was palpable.

Invisible fire.

"God killer," Zorin whispered harshly.

The tip eased forward; Hercules didn't move.

"I touch you, Hercules, and you're nothing but ash. Ash I will ground into the earth with my heel."

Something urgently suggested to Hercules that he figure out what to do, do it quickly, and do it right the first time; there was absolutely no room for mistakes. It also suggested that, in order to be able to do all that, he would have to be alive. It further suggested that, to be alive to do all that, it would be much preferable that he wasn't here, in this tent, with that sword, in the first place.

Hot didn't begin to describe the situation.

"I will give you a choice," Zorin said expansively, pulling the Fire away, aiming the tip upward again. "You can do the cowardly thing and allow me to introduce you to the Fire without opposition. No fuss, no bother. Or, you can allow me to give you a weapon of your own, and we can settle this like the warriors we are. Fuss, bother, and a lot more interesting.''

"That's a choice?" Hercules said.

"It's the only one you're going to get."

Hercules listened to the voices beyond the tent; they were louder now, and he had a feeling Crisalt wasn't going to waste time arguing the fine points, as it were, of the Fire versus a regular blade.

"How about the one where you give me the Fire, I give it back to Hephaestos, and then we discuss what you and King Arclin are trying to do around here."

Zorin was surprised. "Well. Well, what do you know about that." He shook his head in reluctant admiration. "You have brains as well as muscle."

Shows what you know, Hercules thought; if I had any brains, I wouldn't be here.

"Still," the raider said, "it doesn't matter. You won't live long enough to tell anyone anyway."

"You're sure about that."

"Oh, yes. Very sure."

Hercules took a quick step forward, and Zorin, startled, stumbled back, nearly tripping over the first dais step. Once he recovered, seeing that Hercules wasn't about to move again, he sneered, and touched the tip once more to the ground, leaving it there this time, while a column of fire as thin as a blade of grass rose

166

from the earth. It wavered and twisted, and died as soon as the tip was withdrawn.

If Hercules had wanted proof of how a man like this had been able to subdue towns like Drethic without much fuss, he had it now, and wished he didn't.

He also saw something else: that if Zorin persisted, it wouldn't simply be a war against men he would have to fight. Hephaestos could create all the volcanoes he wanted, and it wouldn't make a bit of difference to a man like this.

A madman.

No; the next war would be against the gods themselves, and the gods would be hard-pressed to win.

And when they did win, there wouldn't be much left down here to salvage.

Not much at all.

You know something? Hercules told himself; you think too damn much.

"What will it be?" Zorin asked, arrogance in place. "The hero or the coward?"

Hercules shrugged. "Okay. I'll be the hero. What does that make you?"

Furious, Zorin reared, the Fire poised over his head, and shouted wordlessly as he brought the sword down in a long deadly arc that passed through the space Hercules' head had occupied just before Hercules threw himself to his left, rolled, and darted around to the far side of the pit. The flames there seemed almost a joke compared with the blazing trail Zorin's sweep left hanging in the air.

"You can run, but you can't hide."

"I'm not hiding," Hercules said, shifting accordingly as Zorin moved one way, then the other, trying to force Hercules away from the pit.

"You're right. You can't."

He backed up several steps, and drew a small fire circle in the air. Mocking. Promising.

Hercules braced himself. A man with such pride would not allow this game to continue for very long. He knew what the man thought, and knew that if he moved too soon, Zorin would have him; if he moved too late, Zorin would have him.

What he needed was what he had hoped would have happened minutes ago.

He watched Zorin's legs, saw them adjust almost imperceptibly, and saw the Fire waver as the raider tensed his arm as well.

Close, he thought; it's going to be too close.

"Last chance, Hercules."

"You talk too much," Hercules told him. "If you're going to jump, jump."

Zorin blinked.

Hercules smiled.

Crisalt burst into the tent, a group of men just behind, yelling alarms of escaped prisoners, warning Zorin to be careful, and bumping into each other when they realized that their leader had the escaped prisoner in his own tent, that the escaped prisoner was lunging toward them, that the escaped prisoner probably wasn't a prisoner anymore when he grabbed one of them and tossed him at their leader.

Zorin, enraged by the intrusion and caught by it just as he was ready to take Hercules at his word, dodged the flailing raider hastily, and instinctively held up his hand as the soldier flew at him.

The Fire caught the man's shoulder.

A vivid white light flared and turned red.

The man didn't even have time to scream.

Hercules didn't have time to think.

Following immediately behind the tossed soldier's flight, Hercules ducked his head away from the bright light, and caught Zorin off balance. It was easy to snatch the Fire from his startled grip, a little harder to leap onto the dais and grab the leather sheath, a bit harder still to duck around the fur-covered chair while slipping the sheath onto the blade, and damn near impossible to roll under the tent's edge while lashing out with a boot at Crisalt, who had been the first one to recover.

Once outside, Hercules paused, grateful for the darkness here, and the chance to catch his breath.

When Crisalt's hands poked out from under the tent, ready to pull himself behind, Hercules stomped on them, grinned at the outraged yell, and started to run.

If that was the hard part, this should easy.

All he had to do was run the length of this valley through a camp of soldiers armed to the teeth and ready to kill him, open a fifteen-foot gate that took four ordinary strong men to move, race across the base of a mountain with an army in full pursuit, and find, in total darkness, the entrance to Hephaestos' forge, and thereby save the world in the process.

He could use the Fire, of course, but that wouldn't stop archers or spearmen from taking him at a distance.

Strong he may be, but immortal he wasn't.

The cries of pursuit echoed off the valley walls.

A gong was sounded.

A horn was blown.

The obvious course would be to follow the stream, but that would take him directly through the main encampment; although the torches were placed at far intervals, they wouldn't protect him now as they had before.

There was also the valley walls, but he was no climber, and it would take Hermes, and a dozen like him, to haul him up and out.

And he couldn't let himself forget that this was an army, and Zorin and Crisalt would not let their men run helter-skelter in pursuit. Parties would be organized as fast as orders could be given, and there was no place he could hide that they wouldn't eventually find.

Which left him . . . what?

The horn still blew, and the gong sounded as if it were being beaten to death.

He tucked the Fire more snugly under his left arm and vaulted a pile of rags that had nearly tripped him. An arrow thudded into the ground where his heel had been, and he swerved sharply, changed direction a second time, and headed toward the north valley wall, hoping to lose himself in the warren of tents.

Where the soldiers lived.

Bad idea, he decided, but listening told him that changing direction again would be an even worse one.

His shoulders tensed as he waited for another arrow before he decided that the archer must have loosed the first one in desperation, without careful aim, and that it had landed where it had by simple luck. Otherwise his back would be bristling right now with other arrows.

Ahead he could see men moving, their shadows against the tents, darker forms sliding into the streets between them. Luckily, the full raider complement wasn't here; unluckily, those who *were* here weren't the dregs. If there were any dregs. Which he doubted.

"Halt!"

Two men leaped in front of him.

Hercules didn't stop. He aimed for the one on the right, disconcerting him just enough before charging left instead, bowling the man over before his sword could be used.

Not good, he thought; this is not good.

He heard the second man call for reinforcements.

The gong began to get on his nerves.

They're too focused.

Zorin has trained them too well.

Which suddenly gave him an idea, one he hoped would be the one thing Zorin and Crisalt wouldn't expect.

Still running north, angling now slightly right, he prayed he wasn't making a mistake.

Then he drew the Fire.

17

Men who live orderly lives hate disruption; it's untidy, and probably an unwanted test from the gods that is, all in all, doomed to fail them from the start.

Soldiers who live orderly lives hate chaos. It doesn't fit their lifestyle, and it can't be adequately planned for, therefore it can't be much of a factor in their training. Theory, however, seldom works as planned when reality takes over.

Zorin's initial shock at Hercules' escape with the Fire was undoubtedly long over. Clearly the order to hunt him down had been given; just as clearly, experience would be the soldiers' most potent ally, not to mention their intimate knowledge of the valley and all its cracks, nooks, crannies, and not-so-secret hiding places.

Time, Hercules decided, to give them something else to think about.

He ran up to the nearest tent and slashed the Fire across its side wall. A loud sizzling rose with a stream of dense smoke, and he was startled into an oath when, a second later, the entire wall burst into flame as if it had been made from parchment.

Not bad, Hephaestos, he thought in growing respect for his brother's skill at the forge; not bad at all. Too bad the dope couldn't fashion his temper as well.

He sprinted away and slashed the next tent, grinning at the astonished shouts of alarm as flames coiled brilliantly toward the sky. He skipped the next two as he continued to make his way toward the valley's center, slashed facing tents just as a contingent of spearmen rounded a corner just ahead.

He froze.

They froze.

The tents ignited just as the spearmen charged, scattering them like frightened geese and allowing Hercules to pass among them without having to deliver more than a whack on the temple here and a trip with a boot there.

He would not use the Fire on them; barbarity like that was left to men like Zorin.

The gong assumed a new rhythm, one he supposed meant the place was ablaze.

An understatement.

But at least it wasn't telling them to hunt him down and kill him, if not worse.

He did wonder, though, if the man who wielded that damn beater ever got tired.

He swung sharply left when he came within sight of the shallow stream, had another idea, and forced himself to save it in case he needed something later. Another pair of tents took the Fire's touch before he darted back into the temporary streets, heading west now and letting a long while pass before the Fire spoke again.

And again.

Spreading the destruction out was, for now, his best hope of making sure the troops weren't able to gather in any appreciable strength in any one place; especially not the place where he happened to be. As much as Zorin wanted his head—literally—he also could not afford to lose substantial amounts of his supplies, nor would his men want to lose what little they owned. Discipline, even that born of fear, was already wobbly, if the men he passed were any indication. They barely glanced at him now, too busy trying to put out the flames with buckets of water and wet blankets, or racing around with wildly waving arms as if they could scare the flames to death.

Reaching an open area gave him yet another idea. Low pyramids of barrels were set in its center, and he could smell their contents even at this distance.

A quick smile, another silent promise to return if necessary, and he raced north again.

A tent became a torch.

Two soldiers with solid staffs and soot-smudged faces tried to stop him, but he waved the Fire in their eyes long enough to distract them, then planted one fist against a jaw, another against a cheekbone, and agilely leaped over their sprawled, cursing forms.

It was almost too easy.

A tent filled with grain was the next to burn.

The air roiled with the stench of burning leather, scorched fur, burning cloth and rope and wood. Smoke drifted like mist, obscuring vision and here and there gathering into choking pockets of dense fog.

So far, so good, and he reckoned it was about time to put the last of his hastily formed plan into motion. He still wasn't sure it would work, but it was the only chance he had to survive. If he didn't do this before the fires were under control, Zorin's men would regroup, and they definitely would not be happy campers.

Firelight danced darkly on the valley walls; smoke and fire buried the starlight. It was, Hercules thought, a lot like dropping in on Hades for an afternoon, except Hades was a lot more hospitable. And the food was better, too.

There was no attempt now to hide his destination. He ran straight for it, the Fire at his side, its sheath in his free hand. An abandoned cart had to be veered around, a fallen pile of spears vaulted. A raider knelt near one corner, gagging while tendrils of smoke rose from his back. Another lay prone, half out of an already leveled tent.

Voices stopped him just shy of his goal, and he crouched in the lee of an untouched tent, watching as Crisalt stood near the edge of a small grassy area, pointing this way and that, directing his men to take up their positions and for the gods' sake, will they please forget about the place burning down around their ears and concentrate? Was that too much to ask?

He counted seven, including Crisalt. He had no idea if there were more back there in the dark. And because of the fire, there was not only more light, but the dark areas had become darker, easy enough for a whole squad to hide in if that was Crisalt's aim.

Time, Hercules reminded himself urgently; you have no time, stop thinking and get on with it.

He rocked back and forth, staring at the raider lieutenant, fixing him in his gaze, isolating him and waiting, counting the precious seconds while his rocking grew a little faster, his breathing a little deeper, until he could stand it no longer and exploded from the shadows with a yell that easily overwhelmed the many voices of the conflagration bellowing around him.

Crisalt spun around, sword at the ready.

Hercules saw his lips move, and saw others racing to cut him off. Some were deterred instantly when he dragged the Fire's tip along the ground behind him, spurting flame at his heels; the others came on.

Crisalt stood his ground.

The good part about this was, Hercules knew he wouldn't have to fight all of them.

The bad part was, the ones he did have to fight were too good to be taken for granted.

Off guard again; he had to take them off guard.

Keeping those on his right at bay with the Fire, he slapped the first soldier on his left with the Fire's sheath, and nearly paused to watch when the man was lifted off his feet and flew backward a good ten yards. Well, he thought, that's a new one on me. The next man ducked under the sheath's stinging loop, but in doing so allowed Hercules to smash him with his shoulder. He flew, too, but not nearly as far and not nearly as well.

Crisalt didn't move except to broaden his stance.

Something thudded against Hercules' back, making him break stride and nearly fall. His momentum turned him in a circle, Fire and sheath spinning with him, the latter catching a charging spearman on the hip and tumbling him into a handful of others. They went down with yells and curses Hercules had to admit were, even for soldiers of their ilk, strong enough to burn even Zeus' ears.

Now Crisalt was directly in front of him, sneering as his dagger appeared in his other hand.

Hercules didn't stop, didn't slow, didn't bother to smile when he saw doubt flicker in the man's eyes, then the uneasy glance to either side for support that was apparently too far away for immediate help, then the lips moving in a prayer for courage, then the astonished widening eyes as Hercules continued to bear down on him without even bothering to fake changing direction.

Resigned, Crisalt braced himself.

Hercules left his feet just as the sword drew back, and Crisalt's panicked ducking didn't help—instead of landing on his chest, Hercules' boot caught him neatly on the forehead, toppling him backward with a grunt, forcing sword and dagger from his hands, expelling the air from his lungs as Hercules landed, swept the others back with the Fire, and ran straight over Crisalt's body as if he were a lumpy carpet.

Half a minute later he had reached the corrals. The two drunks were gone, and the horses were in a near panic. They raced around the inside perimeter, eyes white and rolling, ears back. They snorted and whickered their agitation, and as he used the Fire to slice through the thick cord holding the gate shut, he spotted foam on the mouths of some.

The moment he reached for the gate he heard Crisalt's shriek of anger, and the thunderous tramp of many boots heading in his direction.

All right, he thought; change one, sort of.

He hastened to the back, prayed briefly for the animals' safety, then drew Hephaestos' sword along the top rail as he trotted down toward the cattle pen.

A long, too long second passed before the wood became a wall of tall fire; another long second before the horses decided they had had enough. They charged the gate and bulled it open, and immediately began to run in every direction but back.

The second corral was much larger, and its inhabitants much easier to spook. As soon as the rail caught, the cattle and oxen bolted. It didn't matter which side held a gate. They blasted through as if the fence hadn't been there, heads down, horns out, the thunder of their stampede matching the roar of the dozen score fires.

Hercules allowed himself a satisfied smile.

That, he figured, ought to give Zorin's men something to think about.

What he had to do now was get to the gate, and this diversion should give him sufficient time to set the others in motion. This may even be enough, he thought, but he didn't want Zorin to get away so easily. If he couldn't have the man himself, Hercules wasn't about to leave him the camp.

''Hercules!''

It was Crisalt, reeling around the far corner of the corral. From the way his armor was slashed and battered, from the smudges of dirt and smears of blood on his face and bare arms, Hercules knew the man hadn't escaped the entire stampede. As it was, he could barely stand.

"No," Hercules said as the raider staggered toward him. "Leave it, Crisalt. There's no reward for fighting when you can't even hold your sword."

Crisalt spat blood to one side. "You made a fool of me, Hercules. I'm not going to let that go."

A longing glance west toward the gate, a sigh for the man's rigid concept of honor.

He leaned against the end post and waited while Crisalt, threatening all manner of imaginative mutilation and dismemberment, stumbled and fell, rose and stumbled and fell again, rose and stumbled and fell sideways against the fence. Had he been taller, he would have hung over the top rail. As it was, he slid headfirst through the gap.

Hercules blew out a breath and walked over to him, looked down as Crisalt blinked dazedly up.

"I'll kill you," the man said, wheezing.

"Crisalt, why don't you go home?"

Crisalt sat up and frantically slapped the churned earth around him for his sword, or his dagger. "Why should I?"

"Aren't you tired?"

"What of it? I still have to kill you."

"Crisalt."

Crisalt turned, and widened his eyes in an aw,-come-on,-give-me-a-break look.

"If you won't go home, then at least get some sleep," Hercules said kindly, and used his fist to help him.

He figured that was break enough; the alternative was dying.

"Hey! You there!"

Hercules didn't bother to check on the voice's owner. He sheathed the Fire and sprinted away, keeping within the darkness that still huddled at the valley wall's base. By the sight and sounds of it, the search for him had intensified in fervor, more a testament to Zorin's hold than to his men's intelligence.

It wasn't over yet.

18

It didn't occur to Hercules that it was rather odd, there not being anyone around the barrels he had spotted earlier. His first thought was that a fair portion of the men were still hunting him, while the others divided their time between trying not to be trampled by runaway horses and cattle, and not getting scorched by all the fires he had started.

It was too much to hope for that they would all panic and run away.

Still, as he paused for a breath amid the barrel pyramids, he supposed he ought to be grateful for small favors.

Or rather, he amended when he saw the figures drifting out of the smoke, brief favors.

He was surrounded.

He had no idea how many of them there were, but

from their expressions, and the way they brandished their weapons, he had a pretty good idea how angry they were. How murderous they felt. And what they wanted to do to him, as slowly as possible, no matter what Zorin might have ordered.

"Got him!" one of them cried gleefully.

Hercules made an elaborate show of ignoring them as they closed in warily. With one foot he tipped over one of the barrels, then stepped on it to prevent it from rolling away. Once done, he unsheathed the Fire.

The advance halted raggedly as word was passed.

"You can't get us all, Hercules," someone called from his left.

"Some of us, though," another answered nervously.

"But not all," the first one insisted.

Hercules kept his own manner solemn as he turned slowly to make sure they all saw the Fire. Their expressions told him he was probably not giving them enough credit. What they didn't understand was the barrel beneath his foot, and what that had to do with the price of olives.

At least not until a nervous voice said, "Hey. Hey. I think . . ."

Hercules brought the Fire's tip just shy of the barrel head. "Will it burn, do you think?" He studied both sword and barrel closely. "I mean, it works well with lamps and things, but do you think it will . . . ?"

The halted advance sagged in places as several raiders more clever than the others recognized the threat.

"Not to worry," that first soldier said. "It'll just soak into the ground. We won't even get our feet wet."

Hercules didn't think so. The valley's westward slope, gentle as it was, was sufficient to draw the stream from its source and lead it to the pool. The ground itself, especially around here and around the tents, was packed hard as rock. He didn't believe the barrels' contents would simply puddle when spilled.

Of course, there was only one way to find out.

If he was wrong, he was a dead man; if he was right, he might get a little singed, but he'd live a lot longer.

"If we rush him," a voice suggested.

"Well, we're not doing much good just standing around, are we?"

The horn sounded.

The gong sounded as if it had finally developed a crack.

Hercules pushed the barrel ahead of him, kicked it hard, and stove in the side. Oil gushed from the hole, but he was already toppling and smashing as many of the others as he could before the raiders, having had enough, roared and closed in.

In for a penny, he thought, and touched the Fire to the oil.

It didn't look like much—a small blue flame at first, but it spread swiftly, grew rapidly, a rushing sweep of flame that soon turned the roar of attack to the roar of extremely disorganized blame and retreat.

Hercules ran as well. He kept just in front of the onrushing fiery wave, angling sharply to the south as one barrel exploded, sending a brief but spectacular pillar of flame into the sky. Another soon followed, and the flood continued, rushing under those tents that hadn't yet been consumed, seeping into ruts that steered it into more tents, and under wagons, around carts, toward the stream.

It wasn't long before it seemed that every inch of the valley was afire.

The chaos was complete.

No time now for anything but to leave.

And no time for deception.

He ran straight toward the valley gate, ignored by everyone he passed. They were too busy trying to figure out how the earth had caught fire, and too busy trying to figure out how, if the earth had caught fire, they weren't going to.

His next problem was the gate itself, but he figured that after what he had just gone through, that one ought to be fairly simple.

It was.

The gate was wide open.

He grinned, thinking that more than one raider had

hung up his armor for good that night. Even as he approached the exit, he could see a group of them, sacks slung over their backs, racing through toward the plain, followed by a number of horses and one lumbering bull.

The horn sounded, distant and weak.

The gong had shut up.

He slowed a little, pacing himself, the Fire once again sheathed and carried in his right hand. There was no need to wish for light to show him the way— the fire provided plenty, in spite of the rolling clouds of smoke. A glance over his shoulder showed him little else but flame, and dark figures darting from one place to another.

Zorin, he thought, had probably exploded from enraged frustration. He would undoubtedly have to find a new place, a more secure place, to keep his army together. Once, that is, he had gathered enough men to call it an army.

He slowed a little more.

The gate's lintel passed overhead, and his trot slowed again, to a fast walk.

Without the Fire the raider was nothing more than an ordinary bandit with a thirst for blood and money. Not all that big a problem.

He willed himself to go on, that he was just thinking again, and not to pay any heed.

Still . . . Zorin.

Hercules stopped. He stared in the direction of King Arclin's new city, turned, and stared at the fire framed by the gate's massive beams.

No, he told himself sternly, one hand coiling into a fist; you've done what you said you would do. You don't have to do anything else. You really don't.

No one else left the encampment as he watched.

You don't, you know, that silent voice persisted; really, no kidding, you don't have to do this.

"Hermes," he said loudly.

A minute late he snapped, "Hermes, get down here, I know you can hear me."

It didn't take much longer before he heard the flutter of wings, and the complaint that a messenger wasn't supposed to be on call twenty-four hours a day, and who in the gods' name had made that mess in there?

Hercules held out the Fire. "Take this to Hephaestos."

The ground shook as if a great beast walked beneath it. Sparks flared into the night from the valley, and he sensed a light rolling motion beneath his feet.

"Take it. Quickly."

Hermes beamed. "I knew you could do it. Of course, you set fire to half a mountain, but I don't think he'll mind. Boy, are you a mess."

For the first time since this episode had begun Hercules took stock of himself—his clothes were singed, and smoking a bit around the edges, his hair smelled of smoke, his skin felt brittle and cracked, and every muscle in his body complained that it had been wrenched out of place.

"Just take the Fire back," he said impatiently. "With my compliments."

A tall man stood in the gate, hands on his hips, flames writhing behind him.

The ground trembled.

"He's done," Hermes suggested, following Hercules' gaze. "He really is, I think."

Hercules shook his head. "Not yet. He still has men who are foolish enough to follow him. If he doesn't come to an agreement with Arclin, he'll go somewhere else, and nothing will have changed."

Hermes shook the sword. "But he doesn't have the Fire."

"A man like that, he'll find something else."

"So . . . ?"

"So take it away, Hermes. Make Hephaestos happy, keep the lid on, and I'll see you soon." When the sword left his hand, he added, "And don't stop along the way. There is no time."

There was no response but the renewed fluttering of wings.

Hercules walked back toward the gate, where Zorin waited in the fire.

• • •

"You haven't won, you know," Zorin said as Hercules approached. "I'll clean up, get more men, and the first thing I'll do is come after you."

Hercules felt the fire's heat on his face, but the light was still too bright behind the raider for him to see his eyes.

"You've no magic now, Hercules," Zorin jeered. "You're no match for someone who knows how to fight."

Ten yards separated them when Hercules finally stopped, wishing it hadn't had to come to this.

A horse bolted around Zorin and galloped into the night; the man didn't flinch. In his right hand he held a sword, in his left a knotted length of wide rawhide—embedded in each of the knots was a solid metal ball.

"Come and get it," Zorin taunted, smiling to show his teeth. "I have work to do."

He whipped the air lazily with the rawhide and the sword, crossing them over each other, drawing them to his side, crossing them again.

Hercules nodded toward the blaze and the smoke. "You're alone, Zorin."

Zorin scowled. "I don't need them."

The rawhide lashed out, longer than Hercules had thought; he also didn't much care for the whistling sound it made.

"You're not going to win, you know."

Zorin laughed heartily.

"When was the last time you faced someone who wasn't in chains, Zorin? Who wasn't already beaten? Who had something to fight for?"

Zorin didn't answer; he only moved forward.

The sword reflected the fire; the rawhide keened through the air.

"It's pretty sad, isn't it, when you can't even fight your own battles. When you have to hide behind the beaten backs of a hundred men in arms."

Zorin came on, and now Hercules could see his face—it had been severely burned, and was mottled with livid red splotches. Some of his beard was gone, and both his eyebrows. There was filth in his hair.

Hercules rolled his shoulders to keep them loose. "Are you sure you don't want any help?"

"I don't need help," the man snapped.

Sword and rawhide, crossing each other.

"Suit yourself."

The white smile again: "I always do."

Yet Hercules had already seen it, the fury that made the man's limbs a little stiff, the pain that prevented him from complete concentration . . . and the doubt. No one had challenged him like this before, and no one, especially not just one man, had strewn such havoc as would defeat a small army.

That doubt was Hercules' most important ally.

He watched it all build without moving an inch,

hoping his face didn't betray his own nervousness.

Suddenly Zorin boiled over, and charged with an enraged scream.

Hercules easily sidestepped the blind run, tucking away from the reach of the sword and, at the same time, slapping the man's back. Deliberately lightly. Just enough to make him stumble as he whirled to charge again.

This time Hercules took the charge on the rawhide side, using his arm guard to take the brunt of the vicious lash, causing it to wrap around his forearm. The metal balls sparked their own brand of fire, but he yanked the rawhide free of Zorin's grasp, quickly unwrapped it, and tossed it aside disdainfully.

"A mild diversion," Zorin said, panting slightly, swaying to keep on his feet.

"Yes, you are," Hercules told him.

Zorin's eyes widened, his lips drew back, and he came at Hercules in a rush, sword slashing wildly, the tip slicing Hercules at the top of his left arm. Hercules grunted at the pain, instantly buried it, and faced the next rush, this one somewhat less fast, somewhat less strong. The night had tired them both, but Hercules wasn't encumbered by the weight of sword or armor.

Or of mindless fury.

He sidestepped again, and tapped the back of Zorin's skull. Hard enough, this time, to send him sprawling on hands and knees.

192

But he kept hold of the sword.

"Stand still!" Zorin demanded as he stood.

Hercules shook his head. "I don't think so."

But he did.

Zorin charged, the sword only barely held at his waist, and Hercules feinted a sidestep to draw the tip away, then closed with him, hard, slapping the weapon free while wrapping his arms around him. Zorin's momentum took them to the ground, where his frustration gave him more strength than Hercules would have credited him with. They rolled and grappled down the path, Hercules squeezing while Zorin pounded mercilessly on his back and tried to tear out his throat with his teeth.

Smashing into a large bush finally stopped and separated them.

Zorin got to his feet first and aimed a vicious kick at Hercules' stomach. Hercules rolled, catching the boot on his hip, wincing as he sat up on his heels just as another kick came at his face.

He grabbed the ankle, and held it.

Stunned and slightly panicked, Zorin hopped on his other foot and tried to pull free.

Hercules rose.

As he did, Zorin jumped, and twisted, wrenching his trapped leg free while the other whipped around just an inch shy of Hercules' jaw. When he landed, Hercules was beside him. He pulled him up by the scruff, grunted at the wild blows that landed on his sides, and spun the man around.

Zorin saw the apologetic smile, and he saw the fist, and he had no time to react to either.

19

Over; it was over.

Hercules slumped heavily to the ground next to the unconscious Zorin and watched while a few more stragglers made their way out of the valley, toting their possessions, a few herding nervous cattle while a few more rode what horses hadn't already escaped. Only a handful bothered to look in his direction, and only a couple of them reacted when they saw their leader sprawled at his side.

It only took a look to keep them moving.

Over; it was finally over.

Once he realized that, once the adrenaline had stopped pumping through his system and allowed him to think straight, he also realized something else.

He hurt.

He also ached pretty badly, and there were parts of

him he wasn't sure were working the way they were supposed to work.

He didn't have to check to know his arm would be covered with welts from the rawhide lash despite the heavy guard, his back with bruises from the battering it had taken, and the rest of him he didn't even want to think about. Especially the bleeding cut on his shoulder.

The question now was . . . what to do with Zorin now that he had him. To leave him here and let him decide his future for himself was out of the question. Hercules already knew what that decision would be. Killing him would be more permanent, but he had never worked that way; at least not with men. Monsters were something else, and he supposed he should be grateful there hadn't been any of them hanging around this time.

So then, what?

A good strong cell in a nicely maintained dungeon with some helpful but unsympathetic guards for discretionary discipline should do the trick.

Which, of course, raised another problem—which dungeon? Whose dungeon? Whose guards? Who did he trust to continue the raider lord's education in his postwar life?

"You," he said to Zorin, "are more trouble than you're worth."

But a minute later a faint, mischievous smile twitched at his lips.

Two birds with one stone, as his mother used to say; two birds with one stone.

One of them a vulture, the other a rare bird with more plumage than sense.

Groaning aloud to make sure the gods knew he was doing this bit entirely on his own with no help or prompting from anyone, he pushed stiffly to his feet. A check of the valley entrance made him change his mind about going in to find a cart, a horse, even a wandering oxen with nothing better to do. This would have to be a two-foot job.

A loud martyred sigh to make sure the gods understood the sacrifice he was about to make, and he hoisted Zorin over his good shoulder, took a deep breath to get him started, and headed down the slope.

No one stopped him.

One battered and gray-bearded raider, lugging a side of beef on his back and another under his arm, jerked his head toward Zorin. "Dead, is he?"

"No."

"Too bad. You want me to do it for you?"

"No."

"Too bad."

Hercules grinned and moved on.

The weight, distributed as it was, wasn't as heavy as he would have thought. What bothered him was the pokes and prods of the studs in Zorin's armor. When he couldn't stand it any longer, he lowered the man to the ground and unceremoniously stripped him, leaving him wearing nothing more than a wrap of thin leather around his waist for modesty. He also tore from the man's shirt the cleanest strip he could find and wrapped his still-bleeding shoulder as best he could.

Then it was back on his other shoulder for Zorin, and back on the trail.

Sometime later, as the sky began to lighten around the edges of the mountains, Zorin moaned, tried to shift, and froze when Hercules' arm tightened its grip.

"You're hurting me," the raider complained.

"Then go back to sleep."

"Like this? Do you have any idea what I'm going to do with you when . . . where are my clothes?"

Hercules listened for a few minutes while Zorin, having given up all efforts to free himself, instead assaulted him with enough curses to damn an entire continent, enough invective to sear the soul of the most pious of men, and enough inventive threats of applied agony to make the worst of torturers beam with pleasure that the good guys didn't have a monopoly on imagination.

Enough, however, soon became enough.

He stopped, stood Zorin up, braced him upright with one hand, popped him on the jaw without so much as a look or an apology, picked him up, and moved on.

There were, he knew, some things even the son of Zeus didn't have to put up with.

By the time the sun had lifted the top of its arc above the mountain range, Hercules could see the new city spread before him. As much as he still ached, as much as he wished he could stop for a drink of water, he quickened his pace, lengthened his stride, and soon found himself on the road that led to the king's new palace.

Zorin, who had miraculously discovered a way to doze in his position, struggled a little once he realized where they were headed.

"Forget it," Hercules warned. "My knuckles aren't that sore."

Zorin laughed, coughed, laughed once more. "You don't get it, friend. This isn't going to work."

Hercules returned the laugh, but not the cough. "If you think I think King Arclin will release you after I leave, I think you had better think again."

After a moment's puzzled silence, Zorin said, "What?"

Not long after they reached the first of the huts, he gained a following, inquisitive children and curious young men who quickly passed the word of Hercules' prisoner.

Hercules, meanwhile, explained to Zorin that he

had already figured out Arclin and Zorin's plan to expand the kingdom and share the power and wealth. He also explained, since talking helped pass the time, that it hadn't taken him long to figure out how Arclin had achieved his crime-fighting reputation. Which, he added ominously, would not stop; it would just take another, more desirable direction.

Zorin laughed.

Hercules threatened to pop him.

Zorin grumbled into a sulking silence that lasted only long enough for him to overhear the whispered taunts and jokes the ever-growing crowd had begun to make at his expense. His invective returned, but Hercules ignored it, since it only served to make the people giggle, then laugh, then make hasty bets whether or not it was physically possible to do some of the things the raider suggested.

Although there was sore temptation, Hercules refused to smile. The man's humiliation was a bonus to his defeat, yet he didn't want to goad the crowd on by signaling his approval. Sooner or later one of them might remember what they all had had to suffer at Zorin's hands.

That things would get nasty, quickly, was probably a vast understatement.

"I have riches," Zorin said desperately when they reached the open band of grassland between the new city and the palace on the rise. "You can have half."

"Thank you, but no."

"Three fourths, then. I have to have something for my troubles."

"No. I have all I need, thank you."

At the base of the steps he put Zorin on his feet, grabbed him by the nape, and began to climb; the raider, being given no choice, stumbled along at his side.

"This is insane," Zorin snarled. "You don't know him like I know him. You've never dealt with him before. I can tell you now he'll never agree to whatever it is you want."

"Sure he will."

Zorin tried a feeble punch, and had to be held up when an elbow jabbed him none too gently in the ribs.

A crowd had begun to gather at the top of the steps, and Hercules recognized the captain of the guard hurrying down to meet them. The soldier seemed concerned until he realized who Hercules held at the end of his grip, then wavered between terror and abject horror.

"What . . . what . . . ?"

Zorin aimed a slap at Hercules chest. "Kill him, Captain," he ordered. "Kill him." Which would have sounded a lot more impressive if he also hadn't sounded as if he were being strangled.

The captain looked from Hercules to Zorin and

back again, climbing backward as he did since Hercules hadn't bothered to stop. "I . . ."

"The king," Hercules said. "While you're thinking about what you're going to do—and I don't advise you to do it—take me to the king."

"Do and you're a dead man," Zorin swore.

Without breaking stride, Hercules popped him, slung him over a shoulder, and nodded that he was ready now, carry on, I'll just follow along.

The captain, dumbfounded but definitely without the incentive to argue, led Hercules through the whispering members of the court, through the towering gates, and across a broad stone courtyard into the palace itself. They climbed another flight of stairs, marched down a tapestry-lined corridor whose east side was mostly open to the morning, around a corner, another corner, down another corridor, and down another flight of stairs.

"Are you lost?" Hercules asked.

The captain smiled apologetically. "Sorry. I'm just nervous. This is a first, you know."

Hercules stared.

The captain paused, tapped his chin thoughtfully with a finger, then nodded once and eventually led them to a plain, large oak door.

He asked Hercules to wait just a second, pulled the door open, and slipped inside.

Seconds later Hercules heard, "He did . . . *what*? And you haven't killed him?"

This is getting tiresome, he thought, and entered the throne room without an invitation.

King Arclin II, puffed with indignation, sat rigidly on his throne, wearing a voluminous white gown embroidered with blinding silver and tiny gold stars. The captain knelt before the dais, quivering violently.

"You!" the king said, just a half note above a squeak. "How dare you!"

Hercules marched down the center of the room, dropped Zorin beside the captain, stepped up to the throne, reached down with both hands, and picked the king up so that they were facing each other.

The king squawked a garbled order to the captain, who, except for the quivering, didn't move a muscle.

"It's very simple," Hercules said in his most intimidating deep voice. "I know what you've been up to, I know what you two have planned, and you know now that it isn't going to work because I know it, too."

Arclin's face reddened, and his feet kept trying to find something to stand on. "This is . . . I'll have you . . . my people . . ."

Hercules shook him a little.

Arclin sputtered, and his crown fell off.

"How old are you?" Hercules asked, inspiration abruptly drawing the intimidation away.

The king said, "You're tearing my royal robe."

Hercules smiled, and carefully lowered the king back onto his throne. "You're not yet twenty years, am I right?"

Arclin fussed with his clothing, refusing to answer, then yelped, stood, turned and picked up his crown, put it on, and sat again.

"I'll bet your father was pretty hard on you, wasn't he? The old king."

"You can say that again," Arclin said. Then he looked around Hercules and added, "Oh, Captain, do get up. And find some chains for that man there. Big chains. Heavy chains. Really, really heavy chains."

Hercules tapped his shoulder to regain his attention, and the young king started, wide-eyed, frightened. "The people here, they loved him, didn't they? Your father, I mean."

Arclin pouted. "Yes, I suppose so."

"He never had any trouble, did he?"

A moment: "No. I suppose not."

"So you're mad because they don't love you like they loved him."

"Well . . ." Arclin glared, then fell back wearily. "Yes. I try, you know. I want them to have more land to live on, I want them to have more money, I don't tax them all that much . . . and all they ever say is, 'Well, he's not like his father, is he?' all the time. Do you know how frustrating that is?"

Hercules couldn't help a quick laugh. "Believe me, Majesty, I know exactly how frustrating that is."

Arclin frowned, then looked at the ceiling. "Oh. Oh, yes, I guess you might."

The captain and a score of his men returned with enough chain to sink a fleet.

"All right," Hercules said, ignoring the clatter and complaints behind him, "here's how it works, and I'm only going to say this once. Pay attention to what you have and forget trying to take over the world. At least," he added with a wry smile, "for now.

"And stop trying to be like your father. You're not. You're you. Pretty obvious when you think about it, but sometimes recognizing the obvious is the hardest lesson to learn. You do what you think is right, what you think is best for your people, and if your father taught you anything at all, everything will be just fine."

Arclin squirmed. "Yeah. I guess."

Hercules leaned closer, and lowered his voice. "Don't guess. Because if you don't do it, little majesty, I'm always closer than you think."

He smiled, but there was no humor.

Arclin blanched.

The captain gratefully announced that the prisoner was ready for taking to the dungeon.

Arclin looked at Hercules, wondering, then shrugging. "I hate it when I'm not right," he said, although he said it with the ghost of a smile.

Hercules straightened and held out his hand.

Arclin blanched.

Hercules laughed.

The captain, begging enough forgiveness to choke a temple, wanted to know what they should do with Zorin.

A long silence, a longer debate Hercules saw in the king's expression.

Then: "Lock him up, Captain. Lock him up." And he added, "And listen to me very carefully—he will *not* escape. Whoever he once was, he isn't Zorin any longer."

Then he shook Hercules' hand.

A strong grip, Hercules noted with pleasure; the kid will do all right.

Graciously, and with a regret that took him by surprise, he begged off an invitation to a feast the king decided to have that very night, in celebration of Zorin's capture and the end of his reign of terror. There was a long road ahead, he explained, and he wanted to get on it before the sun rose much farther.

"A lady?" the king asked hopefully.

Hercules paused at the throne room door. "No, Majesty, just another promise to keep."

Arclin waved.

Hercules returned the wave and left.

206

* * *

An hour later he found the captain of the guard and said, ''If you don't get me out of this maze, and right now, I'm going to dent you.''

20

That night he camped alone, lying on his back, staring at the moon and the stars. The solitude was wonderful, the fact that he didn't have to do anything, save anyone, fight anyone, was more wonderful still.

He had stopped early, had dozed a while, but the same weariness that weighted his eyelids refused to permit him the sleep he sorely needed.

Which, he thought sourly when something twinged in his left leg, was probably not the best choice of words he could have come up with.

"Lazy, are we?"

Hercules didn't bother to turn his head. "Did you get the Fire back?"

"Has the world blown up?"

"I hope he was properly grateful." He shifted just enough to able to stare at the wings on Hermes' sandals. It was unnerving; in his exhaustion, it looked as if they were staring back. Both the wings, and the sandals.

"He said to tell you he owes you one."

"At least one."

"He's also going to find another summer home. He says that one was too noisy."

Hercules yawned so loudly his jaw popped. And those damn wings were still looking at him.

"And Aphrodite wants to know when you're going to come for another picnic. She thinks she has Hephaestos almost convinced to give this world another chance."

Hercules smiled. "A miracle. I'll go as soon as I can. Next season, maybe."

Hermes leaned over so Hercules could see him. "She'd like that, I think." His expression sobered. "Are you all right?" The face disappeared for a moment. "Gods and little fishes, man, you're not all right, are you? Who dressed this wound here? Disgusting. Where's the ointment for those cuts and scratches?" One of the sandals stamped the ground angrily. "I have never in my life seen a man who needs a nursemaid more. Honestly. Some people."

"Hermes." Hercules yawned again. "Hermes, go. And thank you for all your help."

"No problem. I'd say no sweat, but I just came from the forge. Honestly. Do you think it would kill him to have just one fan lying around?"

Hercules drifted as Hermes went on, thinking it curious that a pair of snakes with nasty red eyes were able to fly in front of him like that. Without wings. A lovely pattern, though. An intricate pattern. Difficult to follow. He must remember to ask them how it was done.

But first he needed to rest his eyes and . . .

. . . when he opened them again, and the sun was up.

The sun was up, his muscles weren't sore, there was no gash on his shoulder, and most of the cuts and scratches had already faded.

By his side lay one of Hermes' special meals, cold but delicious.

"Thanks, brother," he whispered as he took to the road again. "I guess I owe you one, too."

Bestor was the first to spot him as he approached the village; before he had reached the square, he suspected the entire community had left home and shop and farm to greet him. Their effusive thanks was embarrassing, and he was grateful when they finally allowed him to take a seat by the well.

"Bones," Bestor announced, grinning broadly. "I have bones." He reached into the folds of his shirt and pulled out a pair of bones through which a hole

210

had been bored and a leather thong attached. "A toy, see?"

Hercules blinked. "Is that . . . ?" He frowned. "No, it couldn't be." His frown deepened. "It isn't, is it? The bones you . . . ?"

The boy grinned slyly, refusing to admit or deny. "I wanted something to remember you by." He looked away briefly, the toy momentarily forgotten in his lap. "In case you didn't come back."

"Well, I am back. For a while, anyway." He put an arm around the boy's shoulder and gave it a squeeze. "I had to see if you were taking care of your father."

Bestor blushed.

"And," Hercules added, "that you hadn't become an urchin."

Bestor blushed so vividly, Hercules feared the boy's face would burst into flame. He laughed, gratefully accepted a cup of water fresh from the well, and scanned the crowd for signs of Nikos.

"So where is your father?" he asked, thinking it odd the man hadn't come to greet him.

"Well . . ."

A spark of cold grew in his stomach. "He did get back all right, didn't he?"

Bestor nodded. "Yes, sir, he sure did. But he's not here, see, because . . ." He grinned, and pointed.

It was then that Hercules realized that the square

had been decorated with banners and garlands, that there were long tables set around the perimeter, and that most of the villagers were definitely not wearing what they normally would if they had been working.

He frowned. "I don't get it."

A woman's voice said, "Timing, Hercules. It's all in the timing."

Dutricia squeezed onto the bench beside him. She wore a stunning gown of deepest blue, and a neckline that, he noted while trying not to stare, made *plummet* look like an imposter. She giggled at his stricken look, bumped shoulders with him, and said, "Don't worry, it's not for you."

"It's for them!" Bestor cried, fairly bouncing with excitement.

The crowd parted to allow him to see Nikos and Lydia standing beneath the overhang at the inn.

There was no doubt why they were so elegantly dressed.

They waved, and he nodded, rose, and met them halfway.

"It's an honor, Hercules," Nikos said, hugging his new wife to his side.

"No, it's my privilege to be here," Hercules answered, and held up a hand to forestall the obvious questions. "Later, my friend. I'll tell you all about it later."

And he did, and Markan rejoiced, and when the

wedding celebration was at its height, Hercules slipped away. This was no time to claim the attention the couple deserved. He had already promised he would return one day. He intended to keep it.

But for now, neither they nor Markan needed him any longer, and he took the road to the intersection, looked west and decided he had had enough of that for one lifetime, and headed east instead.

He didn't know what was out there, what he would see when the sun rose again, whom he would meet while on the road, but he had no doubt it wouldn't be dull.

He had no magic.

He didn't need it.

Just being Hercules was enough to guarantee the destiny that walked at his side.

On the other hand . . . , he thought when he heard the wings behind him.

"Hercules?"

"Go away."

"I can't. I have a message."

"I don't want to hear it."

"But—"

"Go away. I won't listen."

"But—"

"By the gods, Hermes, haven't you had enough of me for a while? Go. Away."

"All right, if you won't listen to the message—and

I assure you, you'll be sorry, the embellishments are quite good—let me talk to you about that tailor.''

"What tailor?"

"The one who's going to make sure you at least look presentable the next time you have to save the world."

Hercules threw up his hands, and Hermes laughed as he settled beside him.

"You won't be sorry, you know."

"Don't bet on it, brother."

A few yards later he pointed at Hermes. "No kilts, though. I will absolutely not wear a kilt."

"Wouldn't think of it. It's not you. I have seen, however, the most smashing tunic in Corinth. A few alterations, a nip and a tuck, with those muscles you'll look so good I'm speechless already."

"I'm blessed, Hermes. I'm blessed."

"Not while you're still wearing that dreadful yellow."

Hercules laughed and walked on.

What need did he have for magic?

None.

None at all.